WHISPERS
OF THE
DEAD

ADALINE WINTERS

Cover design

by

Liberty Champion

IV

For my daughter,
Your fears will soon become your strength.
Your self-doubt will transform to self-confidence.
As we walk down this scary road, know you are never alone.
I am here for you always.
Mum x

CHAPTER ONE

Vomit, sunglasses and squids.

A lone water droplet slid down the plastic glass containing the scarlet slush masquerading as a Bloody Mary. I bet it the three dollars and twenty cents in my purse that the fifteenth and final guy to grace the chair opposite me would be on the nerdy side. They were nerdy and shy, or so far up their own ass they couldn't see daylight.

I tapped the blunt pencil against the cheap clipboard to the rhythm of Miley Cyrus entering the room on a wrecking ball and glanced at the fourteen 'noes' accompanied by emojis. The first guy spoke in one syllable words and had a vague green tint to his pallor. I'd doodled the sick face with matching vomit. Number six sat like he was making space for the balls of Satan between his legs. He also wore sunglasses in a gloomy room at ten pm. He got the sunglasses emoji. The tenth guy had won the squid emoji, his legs were under the table playing a clumsy and unattractive game of footsie, whilst his hands behaved like spaghetti. That was the longest four minutes of my life. I would kill Sebastian. No car was worth this painful evening.

I sighed and ran through my to do list. At home, the pantry door needed straightening and the porch swing was crying out for a coat of paint and some WD40, so it ceased its incessant whining. That is what I should be doing, not speed dating in the local dive known as The Pit. It wasn't actually called The Pit, but it's what the residents of White Castle called it. Its official name was something flower related... The Orchid perhaps? Or Bluebell? But if you said you were going to The Pit, everyone knew you meant the dive bar opposite the town convenience store specializing in cheap liqueur and knock off perfumes. It boasted terminally sticky floors, served stale beer, and a vague sickly sweet odor clung to the air. The neon street lamps fought a losing battle against the grimy windows, leaving the room sheathed in shadows. It was the kind of place you showered off with a harsh loofah when you got home.

Metal screeched along the cheap laminate floor, which doubled as a dance floor on weekends. The sound set my teeth on edge. The chair continued its protest in a chorus of squeaky plastic as number fifteen took his place opposite me. I squinted at the clipboard and gave myself another three seconds before I won the bet with the cocktail. Three, two... he cleared his throat. I glanced up, irritated at being called out early. My breath caught as I took in a massive man sporting a five o'clock shadow. He was the epitome of masculine, and everything female inside me stood to attention. His muscles bulged under his crisp white Henley as he folded his arms and stared at me. His deep-set hazel eyes studied my face. I blinked, glared at the cocktail and prepared to lose my three dollars and twenty cents.

"Are you going to start or continue to impress me with your one man pencil band?" he rumbled.

My pencil paused, and my gaze snapped to his. A puddle of magic splashed into the surrounding air, the sensation like sizzling rain on my bare skin. Recognizing danger, mine flared in response. I fought it for control. No need to challenge him in a dive bar, how cliché. He narrowed his eyes. I stared at the stupid questions on the clipboard and swallowed. Showing weakness to shifters was like dangling a raw juicy steak in their face and daring them not to shred it. I would not be prey.

"What's your favorite food?" I asked.

"Meat," he growled. I smothered a laugh. Of course it was meat. Served raw and bloody would be my guess.

"What hobbies do you have?"

"Hunting." Uh huh. I bet, just not with guns.

"What were you known for in school?" I squinted at the clipboard. Who the hell thought up these questions? And why was I only now just paying attention?

"Getting what I want." Right, and something told me that was still the case.

"What's your favorite color?"

He gazed into my eyes a beat too long, before scanning down my dress. Stupid low-cut neckline. I would kill Sebastian. "I'm swayed between green, copper and black right now." He grinned, showing me a set of pearly whites

4

and canines a smidge too sharp to be human. I was being treated to his charming side, I'm sure females usually rolled over and showed their bellies when he smiled at them. He leaned forward and caught a curl cascading over my shoulder, pulling it straight. Goosebumps erupted down my arms. "Is that your natural hair color?"

"Yep. Boobs are real too," I said without missing a beat. The idiot glanced at my cleavage. It was a fair question. The deep copper tone looked enhanced, but he should be able to sniff out that no chemicals were used to achieve it. "What's your favorite TV show?"

He released my curl, letting it spring back. "The nature channel."

"That's an entire channel, not a show."

His lips twitched. "Finally, she sways from the questionnaire," he drawled. Placing a giant hand on the clipboard, he pushed it to the table and leaned forward. He could shovel graves with those babies. Or lift a woman and wrap her around him like a burrito. Ugh. He scanned the fourteen noes I'd checked and a wicked grin split his face.

"Nobody catch your eye?" He pointed at the squid. "Not even squid boy?"

I fought not to squirm. "No."

He tapped the number fifteen. "Still?" Arrogant asshole. At least he still fell into one category. Maybe I'll just give the cocktail half the money.

"No."

He sat back and ran a hand through his dark hair, the tips lighter from the sun. His brow furrowed as he regarded me. That's right, I'm not falling for your uncharming ass. Hotness would only get you so far. A golden green rolled over his hazel eyes, so fast if I'd blinked I'd have missed it. But whilst he was assessing me, that move allowed me to peg him.

"Witch," he finally said. Well, if we are going for insults.

"Kitten."

He threw his head back and laughed. The deep booming sound caught the attention of the patrons of The Pit, and a stupefied silence coated the room. Figuring they had heard the practical roar from this male incorrectly, the humans shook themselves and restarted their conversations. It was human nature to rationalize the unnatural, to ignore the impossible, and they were adept at it.

We stared at each other, examining and weighing up strength, intelligence and ability. He was excellent at hiding his alpha status, if not for the unintentional magic splurge; I wouldn't have known he was anything but human. A burly overgrown human with sharp teeth, but still just human. I managed my magic in a similar way. He would assess me as significant, but not a threat.

Never let them see you coming. That was my grandmother's advice, and when you finally showed your cards - be the biggest, baddest person in the room. Own your power and everyone else will follow you. Staring at the guy opposite me, I was sure this master plan would fail. Alphas liked challenges. Whilst I didn't want to be prey, I also didn't want to be a challenge. Indifference was my aim.

The buzzer sounded, signaling the end of this torture. I shot out of my seat and grabbed my borrowed pink Gucci handbag. "Nice to meet you," I said in a weird goodbye. He swiveled in his chair and watched me walk towards the exit.

"The pleasure was all mine," he rumbled. I shot a glare at him over my shoulder, expecting his eyes to be lasered to my ass. His stare collided with mine, I sucked in a breath and thrust my clipboard at Karen, the owner and organizer of The Pit's answer to speed dating.

"No one you like?" she asked, scanning the sheet and glancing back at Mr. Big and Burly. I shook my head, slid one last glance at him and hurried towards the exit as he stalked my every move.

I flew out of the building into the sticky, late summer Louisiana evening and found Sebastian waiting in the silver Bugatti. I flopped into the driver's seat next to him and sighed.

"You made it," Sebastian said with a throaty chuckle, showing he knew exactly how difficult the last few hours had been.

"And you just lost your car for another month."

"At this point you've driven her more than me, it's more your car than mine."

"I don't want your handouts."

"Did you meet anyone?" Sebastian asked, his Nordic blue eyes searching mine.

"I met fifteen someones."

He sighed. "It wasn't meant to be torture, Cora. You were there to enjoy yourself and maybe meet someone worth your time." I spun the car around in the opposite direction and dropped the gear to speed away from The Pit just as the alpha stepped out into the car lot. Sebastian glanced at him, his lean body coiled and a growl curled up his throat. The alpha's eyes flashed cat and a ripple of power skimmed over his flesh. For a second I wondered if he would pounce on the bonnet and challenge Sebastian. That would make for an entertaining end to a dull evening. I subdued an eye roll. Your first lesson, ladies and gentlemen: vampires and shifters loathed each other.

CHAPTER TWO

Eyeballs float—who knew?

It was a well-known myth that vampires couldn't walk in the sunlight, a myth which the vampires gladly fueled. Because hiding in plain sight, or in this case plain sunlight, was the best way to dodge suspicion. Indeed, that particular myth was being dispelled as Patrick Lawrence, the head of house Lawrence, sat regally in the antique armchair in my spacious office at two pm on a bright and sunny day. Facing Patrick was the gracefully graying matriarch of the Wayfer family, Louise Wayfer, who wore a scowl that suggested her wolf was close to the surface. Barry

Wayfer stood at her back with his trembling hands resting on her shoulders, offering his mate support as the two enemies eyed me as if I held the answer to all their problems.

"You're The Undertaker?" Louise asked, gazing at my slight frame. I resisted the eye roll that sat fluttering on my lids as the nickname I'd earned through no fault of my own came back to bite me in the ass. At five foot and a bit to spare, with copper hair and green eyes, I looked more like a flame haired Tinkerbell than a famous wrestler. I leaned back in my chair to put distance between myself and an innocuous heavy thick black bag stretched out on my desk like a sacrificial offering.

"I am. What can I do for you?" I asked both Patrick and Louise.

Louise fluttered her hand towards the bag and held her nose in the air. "We want you to separate them," she stated, still eyeing me as if expecting a more bulky, less dainty version of The Undertaker would tear free of my body.

I raised an eyebrow, wondering if someone had screwed my reputation up from doctor to psychologist. "Who?" I asked.

Patrick leaned forward, grasped the metal zipper of the bag and pulled hard. The links parted, revealing a grotesque pile of remains that resembled something you would put in a stew, not a body bag. All eyes zeroed in on the bag. It was like watching a car crash that's already happened and you're left staring at the aftermath. "Our sons," Patrick offered, sitting back with a frown and folding one smart trouser clad leg over the other.

I leaned forward to examine the contents more closely; I don't know why, it's not like I could discern any parts... oh wait, that's definitely an eyeball. "They are both in here?" I clarified, pointing at the bag.

"Yes, they had a disagreement and sorted it using explosives," Louise stated as Barry drew in a shaky breath.

"I see, and you want me to separate their remains?" I checked.

They nodded as if this was an ordinary Monday morning occurrence. Rubbing my temple, I contemplated how I ended up here. Not here as in this room, here, as in figuring how to separate out vampire and shifter mush. Wow, four years of medical school for this, how the mighty have fallen. I considered my options. No one could ever accuse me of not being a problem solver. "I can't separate them, but I can give you half of their remains, which will only contain your own son."

Patrick and Louise eyeballed each other, and for a terrifying moment I thought they would add to the mush. "This is agreeable," Patrick said, as if there was any other option.

I stood and swiped my hands down my jean shorts. "Excellent."

"When should we return?" Louise asked, patting Barry's hand as he stifled a sob.

"No need, it will only take a few minutes," I stated, zipping the bag up, careful not to touch any mush. I glanced at Patrick and Barry. "Could one of you help me to the clinic?"

"Of course," Patrick said. He stood, flipped his suit jacket onto the back of the armchair and rolled his crisp shirt sleeves to his elbow. He cradled the bag and looked at me, I gestured with my hand for him to follow.

The steel reinforced door in the corner of my office gave way to my lab, which guests rarely saw. I snapped on the bright fluorescent lights and at my direction, Patrick deposited the bag onto the stainless steel examination table. Dragging on a pair of medical gloves, I dug around the bottom cupboard under the sink to find the silver-plated bowl needed for the task. Next I grabbed a plate carved from wood and placed them both on the metal trolley. As I rolled it towards the table, I scooped up a plastic jug. Patrick eyeballed the wooden plate and took a small step back.

"Is that pink ivory?" he asked. Not to be confused with ivory from animals, pink ivory was a rare tree found in South Africa. It was a pretty blush pink color, made the most gorgeous furniture and was lethal to vampires. It was rumored that an ancient tribe blessed the wood to protect them from the obayifo - their version of vampires.

I nodded. "Sure is." Snatching two large clear plastic bags from the drawer, I snapped one open and dropped it inside the scales dangling from the ceiling.

"Are you staying?" I asked Patrick. He nodded, his expression one of morbid fascination. It's a look I'm familiar with. Adding together the estimated weight of an adult shifter and an adult vampire, I scooped up the mush using the jug from the table into the scales. Satisfied I had approximately half, I removed the bag, replaced it with the empty one and repeated the process. The final few grams I separated equally. Then I tipped the contents of one bag into the metal bowl. The remains hissed and protested as vapors poured from the bowl. Years of obnoxious smells have made me immune to their vulgarity, but judging by the pastiness of Patrick's face, it wasn't pleasant. Just as I was about to tip the other bag onto the wooden plate, Patrick reached out and touched my arm.

"Wait, the eye is most definitely my son's." He pointed to a blue eyeball swimming at the top of the bag, I'm slightly fascinated by the way it's causally bobbing on the top of the mush. Should eyeballs do that or should they sink? This is why I have no friends. I fished it out and plonked it into the metal bowl. Nothing happened. *Cora Roberts - rescuer of eyeballs.* I repeated the process with the wooden plate until I was left with two steaming bowls of uncontaminated supernaturals, one vampire, the other shifter.

I glanced around my clinic and realized I had nothing large enough or leak proof to deliver the remains back to their respective families. They couldn't have the bowl or plate. The bowl was expensive, and the plate was rare and in demand given that it was made from the only substance known to kill vampires—well, other than explosions, apparently. I believe decapitation was also an issue. I grabbed my phone from my shorts pocket and zipped off a text. Patrick shoved his hands in his pockets and glanced around the makeshift cold and clinical lab I'd set up. It had started off as a basic doctor's examination room. Over the years I'd added to it with a body sized refrigerator and an x-ray machine. We don't wait long until Maggie bounds through the door, arms full of Tupperware containers.

"I wasn't sure which ones," she rushed out as her collection clattered to the side. She crept closer to the table, her nose wrinkled in disgust. "Ew…" I'm teaching her tact, though not very well it seems.

"Thank you, Maggie," I stated, staring at her. She got the hint and skipped out of the room. Picking two equal sized tubs, I tipped the contents of the shifter into one, and the vampire into the other. The eyeball swirled around on the top, before winking below the mush in a macabre goodbye. I doubt my aunt had this in mind when she bought out the Tupperware party years ago. Securing the lids, I handed Patrick his remains.

"That was… erm… economical."

My gloves hit the yellow bio waste bin with a slap, as I usher him back towards my office with the other tub in my arms. "Thank you, Mr. Lawrence." *I think.*

Louise stood and smoothed her hands down her modest charcoal pencil skirt. Barry stepped forward with his arms stretched out. I guided the tub into his arms.

"You can pay Maggie upstairs when you leave," I explained, ushering them out, that was an easy but weird job.

A scattering of paperwork and bills had my attention when a loud bang snapped through the air, causing me to drop my pen. What now? I jogged up the stairs to find my longest staying resident staring out the west-facing window, shamelessly curtain twitching.

"What is it?"

Rebecca turned to me with a perfectly plucked, arched brow. "Our neighbors seem to be having domestic problems."

I groaned and stalked out through the front door and onto the porch to investigate. Paul and Janet Robinson had been renting the converted stables on my land for the last three months. They were quiet and paid on time, the perfect tenants. Rebecca joined me on the porch and leaned over the banister with a disinterested expression.

"You cheating ungrateful lazy mutt," Janet shouted as a bulging brown leather suitcase went flying from her hands into the back of a banged up pickup truck. She swung around to face a wide-eyed Paul who held his hands up in surrender. She caught sight of us gawking, her gaze narrowed on Rebecca and she reached into the pickup and swung a shotgun in our direction.

"What did you do?" I muttered.

Rebecca shrugged and flipped her ice-blonde hair over her shoulder. "The boy was starving for affection."

"And you gladly gave it to him?"

"He gave back," she said with a wink.

"I remember specifically having a discussion with you about not seducing my guests."

"They're not guests, they're tenants."

I rubbed my left temple, staving off the migraine that had been threatening to appear since the black bag opened on my desk. A shot sounded a split second before a scattering of chalky dust burst from the white wall behind me. Great, something else that needed fixing.

"She's a poor shot." Rebecca noted with detached nonchalance, which for her was easy to pull off given the bullets wouldn't kill her. Me however...

"You man robbing, blood sucking whore," Janet screeched, hitting tones which would cause dogs to howl. I winced.

Rebecca sighed. "The insults are so obvious these days. Nobody puts any effort into intellectual threats and witty comebacks."

"You're a lost cause," I deadpanned.

"Maybe I should attend a help group?"

I snorted. "The last thing you need is to be placed in a group of sex addicts. It would be like taking a bottle of whisky to an AA meeting."

Janet's slurs become crasser and would burn the ears of a sailor. Paul, the coward, jumped into the truck and started the engine.

Rebecca wrinkled her nose. "You smell of charred meat." Rebecca, everybody, the only vegetarian vampire in existence.

"That's what happens when you are gifted with the guts of a vampire and a shifter, then asked to separate out their individual tissues for appropriate burial."

Rebecca's brow furrowed. "How did you manage that?"

"Halved the remains, put one batch on a silver plate and the other on a pink ivory plate."

"You own a pink ivory plate? Should I be afraid?"

"Depends whether you listen to me and stop seducing the guests."

Rebecca chuckled. Janet strode closer.

"Put the gun down, Janet," I said.

She swung the gun to the right, more in my direction.

"And you, you stuck up witch bitch, putting up with the vampire slut." Her arm tensed and shoulder straightened. That's quite enough. I called on my element, the sensation like breathing the cleanest air you could imagine. My magic sought the closest source of water, the Mississippi River, running along the rear gardens. The sheet of water came riding around the corner and halted in front of the house. I rotated my right arm and bent the liquid to my will. It whipped around, creating a translucent shield and forcing Janet to step back. The whole thing took less than two seconds. A shot fired, the bullet lodging in the water. Reaching forward, the water formed a hand stretching back to me, allowing me to pluck out the still warm bullet.

"Hand," I said to Rebecca. She gave me her palm with a tiny scowl on her delicate features.

I dropped the bullet in her palm. "A souvenir of your time with Paul, and a reminder not to sleep with other women's males."

Paul revved the engine, then honked the horn. Janet threw the gun on the lawn with a growl, stomped to the truck and dragged Paul out by the scruff of his neck. He landed on the lawn with a yelp. Janet jumped in, floored the pedal to metal and peeled out of the driveway and onto the main road without pausing. Luckily for Janet, White Castle was a small town with less than two thousand residents, so despite it being a main road, traffic was always light.

Caught in the sitcom that is Paul and Janet, Rebecca and I turned to watch Paul pick himself up with slumped shoulders and drag his feet inside the house. He glanced over his shoulder with a puppy dog look at Rebecca.

I sent the water towards the citrus trees and released it; the summer was proving to be a cruel one, even by Southern standards. "Uh oh, you might have a shifter stalker in the making."

"He knew the score, I'm like the opposite of that saying they use at Christmas."

My fingers drummed on the banister as my brain scrambled for what saying she was referencing. "Peace to you and your family?"

She shook her head. "I'm just for Christmas, not for life."

I chuckled under my breath and turned, sidestepped the porch swing, and reentered the house. "Wow. Just wow."

She followed on my heels. "Speaking of men, how did your speed dating at The Pit go?"

"Sebastian's Bugatti is mine for another month."

She chuckled. "I knew you'd get through it, you love that car. What I meant was, did you meet anyone?"

My mind flashed to the enigmatic shifter. "They were either too quiet and shy, the type I would eat for breakfast, or arrogant and cocky, the type I would most likely kill on a first date."

Rebecca huffed. "Your standards are too high."

"At least I have standards," I muttered.

"You have a 'back off or get bitten' vibe that most men would run screaming from."

I spun and grinned. "And if they stick around after that vibe, they might be worth investigating."

"Out of fifteen guys, not one of them caught your interest?"

I frowned. "There was an alpha."

A wicked smirk pulled at her lips. "Oh, really?"

"But he was too self-assured, arrogant, cocky even. I can't date someone who thinks they are prettier than me."

"So he was well groomed? That's his crime?"

"No… he called me a witch."

Rebecca sucked in a breath. Elementals are born with links to the elements, a direct line to the magic shrouding the Earth. Witches are humans who dabble in magic, mostly they make useless potions and pray to a nonexistent deity. It was an insult.

"What did you do?" she asked.

I shrugged. "Called him a kitten."

Our joint laughter echoed around the house.

CHAPTER THREE

Secrets are like onions.

Summer Grove House was a white-washed plantation house erected in the Pelican State of Louisiana by my ancestors in 1793. Following costly damage courtesy of Hurricane Gustav we were forced to diversify our business. Even the general upkeep of the four-story building was more than the bed-and-breakfast was making on its own. The basement now housed my office, unofficial lab and clinic, suited specifically for the supernaturally inclined. We specialized in loners; supernaturals not affiliated with a vampire house or a shifter pack. The ground floor was the communal living area and kitchen. The first floor contained guest bedrooms, and the converted attic housed my private quarters.

Supernaturals fell into three distinct species; vampires, shifters, and elementals. Elementals were the most integrated into human society, yet considered the furthest from them. A government ruled them, The High Order of Elementals (THOE), commonly known as The Order. Unlike shifters and vampires, you didn't opt in; they ruled you regardless as to your personal views – a little like humans and their presidents and prime ministers. In theory, voting was fair and unbiased. In reality, it was a popularity contest. Of course like any parliament the leader drove the flavor of the views, and for the last twenty-two uncontested years it had been a tyrannical bitch with elitist views. Elementals stuck to their family groups, similar to covens, except we didn't do any of the creepy crap human witches seem to have adopted. All elementals had an affinity; earth, water, fire or air, and all could learn basic magic skills, locator spells, etc. Approximately ten percent of elementals had a secondary gift, and of those ten percent, one percent were psychic. Most psychics were precogs with their visions and intuitions based on events in the future. I was a retro, my gift was focused on the past, specifically death. With these secondary gifts came a price, the universe taking its pound of flesh. For me when I touched someone to glimpse their last moments, I was forced to relive their soul crushing fear and terrible pain. Speaking of the dead, I pointed at the familiar Tupperware perched on the rectangular reception desk as my sandals slapped against the wooden floor. "Why is that still here?" I asked Maggie, who was currently swinging on the chair and filing her nails into sharp points with intense concentration.

Maggie blinked at the plastic tub like it was a surprise. I'd been accused of being a sucker for a sob-story, and Maggie was living proof of that. A lone bobcat shifter on the run from an abusive father and an arranged marriage, she turned up on my doorstep when a local shifter family took pity on the bruised and beat up girl. That was a year ago, and since then Maggie has blossomed into a cute but clueless girl who I let live here rent free in exchange for her work as my receptionist and general help. I tapped the top of the plastic to get her attention.

"Maggie, why have the Wayfer family left their son on my reception desk?"

She pulled at one of her dark pigtails and smiled, her chocolate brown eyes lighting up her face. A native American beauty, in a few years I would need to bat off any unmated male in a hundred-mile radius. "The woman said she doesn't have room to bury her idiot son in the family plot. He didn't even leave her any grandchildren, so she paid the extra for us to take care of him."

Right, the Wayfer's were loners, living outside of pack politics and protection. I dimly recalled they lived on the east side of town in a small two up two down with a garden you could barely swing a cat in. "There's a prepared plot under the Magnolia trees on the South side. Would you take care of him?"

She nodded, grabbed the tub like it contained her lunch and not somebody's son, and trotted out the side door towards the burial fields. I felt around under the reception desk for the garden plans. I kept a concise map of everybody's whereabouts should some wayward family come seeking the remains of their kin. My pen paused over the plot I'd sent Maggie to. Damn, I didn't know his name. I

28

marked him down as Wayfer son with today's date. I forewent gravestones as I didn't want to advertise that I allowed shifters and vampires to be buried in my garden. That would be hard to explain to local human law enforcement.

I thought of what awaited me in my room, and with a resigned sigh climbed the three flights of stairs to the attic. Whilst my elemental magic cost me little, this next part would cost me at least a few hours of sleep, and several hundred calories of which my waistline was eternally grateful. I passed an aging vampire couple strolling down the hall arm in arm. They had been here for two nights, Lillian and Stephen Graham. Lillian was a slender woman, with deep auburn hair, she wore blue dress trousers that matched her eyes with a cream blouse. Stephen was clad in corduroy fawn trousers and a green shirt. He wore his dark blonde hair slicked back. I believe they were visiting their newly born grandson. Their daughter had married into a house, but their loner status meant they could visit, but not stay. Vampire politics suck. Maybe that should be their motto? Stephen nodded towards me, whilst Lillian gave me a beaming smile. "Thank you so much for giving us the room

29

in the West Wing, Cora, it has the most beautiful sunsets."
She gazed at Stephen like the sun rose and set with him, not
the East and West.

"You're most welcome, Mrs. Graham, I hope you'll
consider us next time you have cause to visit White Castle."
Satisfied customers meant repeat business, and that's what
Summer Grove needed. We were barely holding our heads
above water, and at less than forty percent occupancy, I had
a supernatural bed-and-breakfast business to grow. The
Graham's held on to each other as they gracefully descended
the stairs to the ground floor, meanwhile I dragged my tired
ass to my white double doors and exhaled as I pushed it
open to find the Wayfer's son sitting on my sofa looking
confused as hell.

Having a secondary gift was both a blessing and a curse.
A blessing because I was graced with extra magic, cursed
because the gift wasn't returnable and you couldn't unplug it
when you'd had enough. I tipped my head at him as I

opened the refrigerator and grabbed a Gatorade. I needed hydration and calories for what was coming. Cracking the top, I took a long swig and wiped the slight dribble with the back of my hand along with half the pastel pink lipstick I'd worn this morning. "What's your name?" I asked the Wayfer's son.

He squinted at me. "Tom Wayfer. Wait, you can see me?"

I nodded. Oh boy, he'd figured out nobody could see him—I tried to get to them before they could freak out. "Tom, your parents brought you here after you had an accident-"

He jumped up and rushed towards me. "It was no accident, Mario promised me an honorable fight and the conniving bloodsucker tried to ram C4 down my throat." He tried to slam his fist against the marble counter and succeeded to freak himself out further when it disappeared inside my canned goods cupboard. He pulled his fist out and blinked at it as if to wish it back corporeal. Oh Tom, if only it worked like that. In life, Tom had been a lean guy with cropped dark hair and a builder's tan. The crinkles around his eyes suggested laughter was found and shared easily.

"He succeeded," I pointed out, willing away the belch stuck in my throat from guzzling the Gatorade.

Hard ice-blue eyes turned on me, reminding me that shifters have an animal side that, no matter the species, one should not mess with. "No, before he could, I grabbed the bastard by his balls and tried to ram it down his throat." Lovely imagery. Thanks Tom, I'll sleep better tonight.

"Let me guess, it exploded before you could get away?"

He nodded and stared around the open plan living space. I'd made my apartment light and airy, taking advantage of the many floor to ceiling windows. The furnishings were in neutral shades of cream and sky blue. It was somewhere one could easily meditate, if I could find five minutes to myself that was.

"Why am I here?" he asked.

I hated this part, the one where the soul in question expected to be at their own family plot on their own lands—nobody explained it to them, and those responsible left before giving the bad news. It was a constant reminder that family could be ruthless and cold. Death sometimes brought out the worst in people. "Your parents felt it best that you be laid to rest here at Summer Grove House."

"The creepy plantation owned by 'The Undertaker,'" he scoffed and air quoted my nickname, "that talks to the dead?" I waited a beat to see if he would catch on. He stared back at me. Nope, clueless as they come. Seems he had nothing between his ears even before the explosion.

"That would be me."

He threw his head back and laughed. I hated that nickname. Even the dead found it hilarious, and they were on the blunt end of my gift. When I find out who started it, I'd make them pay.

"Wait, if I'm not buried on family grounds, I won't get my rites and join my ancestors. That malicious bitch." I assume he meant his mother and not me. It was cruel to damn their son to an eternity of wandering the earth, but I had a solution that eased my guilt over offering my own gardens as a graveyard for those least wanted.

"If you follow me, I can explain," I said, stepping around him. I could just walk right through him but that would be impolite, also it gave me the chills. I made my way across the wooden floor, which I'd made a feature throughout the house, and headed towards the faded white door in the center of the far left wall. Secrets were in layers, and the

33

closer you got to the center, the fewer people knew. There were the ones you told acquaintances to break the ice, like your favorite movie being a spoof comedy that would often feature in one of those guilty pleasures lists. Then there were the ones you told your friends, like having a crush on someone or not answering the phone when your grandmother calls. The penultimate were those secrets that you held close to your heart, it was often knowledge that someone could use to hurt you and somebody either knew that secret by circumstance or because you had trusted someone enough with your heart. Finally, there was a secret you told no one through fear of the consequences, these were the secrets you daren't breathe to a single soul because that knowledge wouldn't hurt you, it would be your destruction. I hid my ultimate secret behind this door, not another living soul knew about it. Grasping the ornate silver key hanging on a long chain from around my neck, I pushed it into the lock, chanted a quick uncloaking spell and pushed open the door.

CHAPTER FOUR

I specialize in bones, not brains.

"Where in the bloody Nora has someone hidden the lemon cookies?" I muttered, shoving the small stool along the tiled floor with my foot until it hit the corner cupboards. I stepped onto it, arched to my tiptoes and felt along the top of the kitchen cabinets. My hand grazed something ceramic, bingo. The phone erupted in my shorts pocket, the annoying melody punctuated with a rhythmic vibrating—just to ensure I couldn't miss the call. My hand trembled as I dug around in my shorts. After passing out for twelve solid hours, not my normal three after dealing with a soul, I was in desperate need of sugar. I put it down to the previous twenty-four hours being a crazy mix of business issues. Separating vampire and shifter remains was the least exhausting, and Rebecca's tryst gone wrong had been the least eventful. After ten torturous hours of labor—well, it looked torturous, I helped the Andersons deliver four beautiful bear cubs into the world. On my way home, Lloyd, the town drunk, drove his truck into a lamppost, but not before hitting Macie, a twenty-year-old wolf shifter with a temper like a Tasmanian devil. She exploded into fur, a common reaction to help her heal, but also to rip Lloyd's throat out. I saved him from certain death, and her from exposure just in time with a well-placed dart in her hind leg, and an equally well placed spell on his memories. I'd then reported him to the sheriff's department, waiting extra time to speak to the sheriff in person. He was obnoxiously determined, and I could count on him to ensure they dealt with Lloyd.

"Cora Roberts," I answered just as my other hand grasped the jar. I gave a tiny yelp as I claimed my prize and stepped down.

"What are you doing?" a guttural voice asked. Dave or 'Dangerous' Dave, as those in the know called him, had deemed to call me. I sighed. There goes my quiet morning. Unlike me, Dave lived up to his nickname. He was the pack's chief enforcer, protector of the Principal and master of all things security related. Three years ago, I'd been running the bed-and-breakfast for four months, when one of my guests, a lone Fox shifter called Boris, was found dead face down in the bed. Fun fact about shape shifters, if they die mid-shift they stay that way. Orange fur erupted like tufted flames over his body–everywhere. I'd seen some interesting stuff as a doctor, but at the time that topped my weird shit list.

It wasn't like I could call the authorities or even the guy's family. He had none. So I called the pack, and that was how I met Dangerous Dave and soon after became his unofficial lone shifter coroner. If a loner died in the area, Dave sent them to me to check if it was of natural causes. It almost always was, and if it wasn't, it was because they'd gotten into a fight. Either way, unless the fight was with a pack member, it wasn't Dave's problem. But he was meticulous and busy— so he outsourced. I wasn't complaining; it boosted my earnings and gave me breathing room whilst I built up Summer Grove's reputation.

"I'm about to eat some cookies," I stated, popping the lid of the jar. I reached inside. "No way," I whispered.

"What's wrong?" he asked.

"Someone ate all my cookies," I seethed as my sugar levels tanked in outrage.

"Eat an apple or drink some juice," he suggested. Nutritional advice from someone who only ate greens if their meat got caught in the grass during a kill. I yanked open the fridge door and guzzled the orange juice from the glass bottle. At least it was freshly squeezed. "Better?" Dave asked. I blinked, my brain focusing a little more. He might not know the specifics of my abilities, but he knew the aftereffects of my using them.

"Yup."

"Who died?"

I sighed. "The Wayfer's son, Tom, and Patrick Lawrence's son."

"The Wayfers over on East?" Chief enforcer equaled nosy busybody that made it his business to know everyone else's, pack or no pack.

"Yup."

"And Patrick Lawrence of House Lawrence?" he asked carefully. He was weighing up how much backlash might occur.

"Yup."

"How?"

"C4."

He chuckled. "Huh, figures." I don't even want to know.

"What can I do for you?"

"I got one for you, Cora. Drop off in an hour?"

I slid onto the cracked wooden bench surrounding the kitchen table and grabbed a cream pad and a neon pink pen with a springy feathered flamingo on the end. "Name?"

"No."

"Species?"

"No."

"Age?"

"No."

"Are you going to communicate in more than monosyllables?"

A beat of silence. "No."

I sighed. "Fine, one hour. I should be able to assess them this afternoon."

"Why, what are you doing this morning?" Oh, I'm sorry master, should I move my entire life when you ask me to do something?

"Eating breakfast, fixing the bullet hole in my front wall, and speaking to my residents about the virtues of being virtuous."

I think it said more about me than him that he didn't question why I would have bullet holes in my wall. "I see, well could you make it a priority after you've finished devouring every sweet thing in the kitchen, putting a bit of putty in the wall and having a pointless conversation with Rebecca on not seducing the guests?"

"What's up? You aren't normally a hard ass on a time constraint."

He sighed, the weight of the world on display in one breath. I wonder if they paid him enough? "It's the Pack's quarterly social tonight." Ah, that would do it. They invite every shifter family in the area to a meeting located somewhere deep in pack territory, fueled with pheromones, booze, and tempers. I'd heard the rumors, and if they were

40

true, it would be likely Dave would have more than one body to deal with before the day was over.

"Good luck," I told him.

"Thanks. I doubt there will be anything, but let me know the verdict on the loner."

"Sure." The phone went dead. I blinked. Dave wasn't a talker, but he also wasn't rude—must be the pack social. I'd aim to have his loner evaluated before dinner time. That meant a little multitasking was in order. Rebecca swanned into the room, looking ethereal in a gauzy ivory gown with her flowing blonde hair trailing down her back. I'd planned to eat whilst filling the bullet hole, but this would do.

She smiled as she pulled open the refrigerator door and selected the honey, fresh fruit salad and yogurt. "Good morning, Cora. Would you like some?" she asked, her hands paused at the cupboard with the bowls.

I nodded. "Please. Let's talk."

She glanced up from her assembly of the healthy breakfast bowls. "Uh oh, I sense a Cora lecture."

I smiled and waved my hand towards the opposite side of the table. She released a gigantic sigh and placed the bowl which looked yummy in front of me. Then took my

41

invitation to sit across from me. "Why do I feel like a naughty teenager about to be told off by her mother?"

I lifted an eyebrow. "Perhaps, because you're acting like one?"

She shrugged and deposited a dainty amount of fruit in her mouth. Meanwhile, I shoved two spoonfuls in mine. Low blood sugar waited for no one. If I didn't eat soon, I'd crash again. "You're over a hundred years old. You must know having sex with someone else's mate, partner, husband, boyfriend, or whatever other label you want to attach to it is wrong."

She crossed her legs and chewed her fruit. Offering me a small smile after she'd swallowed. Like Dave had pointed out, it wasn't the first time we'd had this conversation—nor did I doubt it would be the last. "I have limited choices." Also true, Rebecca stayed in the house, or on the grounds all the time for her own protection. I scoffed.

"Would you like me to order an escort service?"

Her amber eyes danced with amusement and interest. Oh, me and my stupid sarcastic mouth. "That would be one solution." I don't think so...'The Undertaker' nickname had done enough damage. What on earth would they call me if they thought I was running a brothel?

"No, I was joking."

She shrugged. "There are other solutions."

"Like?"

"You could hold a singles night at the house."

I pinched the top of my nose. Why me? "Like speed dating for the supernatural singletons?"

"We already have a monthly bingo night, karaoke night, and BBQ party."

Maggie bounced into the room, offering us a serving of her good morning and perky attitude. It had taken me months to get her to this stage—but then she took off as if this is the person she was always meant to be. I didn't have the heart to dampen her spirit, even if it gave me a headache looking at her when I felt like death warmed up. She dropped an empty Tupperware box in the sink.

"Is that my Tupperware tub?" I asked, pointing at the familiar box.

Maggie glanced up from her phone. "Hmm, yes - who else's would it be?" Teenage sarcasm - save me now.

"I'll rephrase. Is that the Tupperware tub that contained Tom Wayfer?"

She blinked. "Yes, you told me to bury him."

"What did you bury him in?"

Please don't say the ground, please don't say the ground. "The ground," she supplied. Of course she did.

"So you tipped Tom's remains into the ground, and what? Just covered him up with muck?"

"Yeah, what did you want me to cover him with silk and lavender?" The lavender might help. The reason we bury our dead in caskets and urns is to protect them from 'evil' spirits. Shifters, like elementals and vampires, held residual magic even after death, and a nasty experience with a sloppy burial a few years ago taught me to never skip this step. Digging up the plot at this point was useless, his remains would have already seeped into the ground. It would be impossible to get all of them back in the tub. I just had to hope no nasty critters using dark magic were around.

"What are we planning?" Maggie chirped.

"A singles night," Rebecca said and I shot her a frown. She smirked like the cat that got the cream. Awesome. Rebecca knew I had trouble saying no to Maggie.

Maggie squeezed her hands into fists, jumped up and down and squealed. Great, now it would be like taking candy from a child... on its birthday.

"I'm not sure-" I started.

"Oh. My. God. This is going to be amazing. The local loners will go crazy for it. We could have cocktails and a different theme every month. Oh, I can make those new canapés I was trying out." Wow, if the guests didn't kill each other, Maggie's cooking would. Rebecca wrinkled her nose, no doubt remembering Maggie's attempt at vegetarian jambalaya last week. My taste buds still craved milk to scour the taste from their poor burned surfaces.

"We could spend this afternoon planning," Rebecca said with a wink.

"Count me out, Dave is sending over a body," I said, shoveling the final spoonfuls of yummy fruit in my mouth.

"He sends you the sweetest of presents," Rebecca said.

"That's okay, Cora," Maggie stated, "leave it to me and Rebecca. We'll plan a party worthy of an article in the White Castle Chronicle."

I hid my wince. "Keep it low key, we don't want to attract any humans."

"Sure thing, boss. And I'll bake some extra cookies for later this afternoon."

Now cookies were one thing this girl could make. I gave her a genuine smile as I stood and stretched my arms up. The doorbell rang, carrying its merry tune to our group. I groaned. It hadn't been an hour, so it wasn't the body, and Dave always used the underground garage to drop off bodies.

I trudged up to the front door, the lace curtains obscuring the visitor. I flung it open. Paul waved some bills in my face. "This month's rent, Cora," he said, looking over my shoulder, his eyes wide as he searched for the ice princess. Too bad buddy, she was a one-night wonder, and she always warned them. Yet it was every man's belief they would be the one to turn Rebecca's head and make her fall in love. Idiots.

I took the money, and he shoved his hands into the back pocket of his jeans and glanced at the floor. "I'm leaving, I can't afford the rent on my own. So that's for the last month, I'll be gone by the end of the week." Great going Rebecca, now I had an empty property for rent. That speed dating scenario was looking more likely.

I leaned against the door frame. "She isn't coming, Paul."

He glanced over my shoulder again and sighed. "I know, she warned me."

"I'm sorry about Janet."

He snorted a laugh. "I'm not, she was a malicious back stabbing bitch. She slept around with anything with fur."

I blinked. Again, I wondered if I got confused with a psychologist. Got a broken bone? I can set it. Got a headache? I can treat it. Got a dead body? I can tell you how they became deceased. Got a relationship problem? I was not your woman. Not only was my attempt at relationships disastrous, I flavored my advice with distrust and heartache.

"Okay," I said. Nice save Cora.

He frowned at me. "So I'll head out tonight then."

I nodded. "That would be best."

His face crumpled. Somewhere in my medical training I was aware this is where I should comfort someone, but I had nothing to give a man that slept with another woman and used it as an excuse to exit his abusive relationship.

He turned, shoulders slumped, and shuffled off the porch and down the steps. Rebecca appeared at my side. "He's sad," she observed.

"At this rate, I'm going to need to section off part of the garden for all these broken hearts you keep leaving at my door."

CHAPTER FIVE

Gifts, deals and favors.

The inconspicuous black van rolled backwards into the spacious underground garage. Dangerous Dave jumped out of the passenger side before it stopped moving, clad in his trademark black jeans and matching plain T-shirt. Flecks of grey speckled his dark wavy hair, showing his age to be at least one hundred, but he was still fit, with a muscular but lean body. Another fun fact about shifters: they live a long time. Two hundred and fifty years old was about average.

He nodded at me as I reached for one of the rear doors and he grasped the other. "Cora, how's business?"

Translation, could he push my fee down further because I'm desperate? "Good, we have bookings all summer long."

He nodded. "Long term, visiting relatives or vacation?"

Translation, who is staying in my town and what motives do they have? "A mixture," I said as we rolled the body bag onto the waiting stretcher. Dave huffed out a laugh. He knew I'd tell him anything the pack's head of security needed to know, but I protected my residents' privacy and he knew it.

I grabbed hold of the stretcher and backed into the unlocked metal door, using my butt to push it open. Dave followed me at the other end. A ball of snowy white fur shot out of the van between my legs and into my lab. I arched an eyebrow at Dave.

"What the hell was that?" I asked.

He glanced around the room, seeking the furry menace. "A cat, she was perched on this guy when we found him."

"I'm not a pet shelter."

He shrugged. "Me neither."

"Dave," I warned as we lifted the bag onto the metal slab. I grunted with the effort whilst he looked like he was moving a bag of sugar. Shifters and their stupid supernatural strength. "Consider her an extra perk of the job."

I glanced around the room, finding the fluffy white cat with calculating cerulean blue eyes studying me from under the metal slab her former owner rested on. I tilted my head; she narrowed her eyes. Hmm… I don't do pets, apart from the goldfish that Maggie had won at a visiting fair six months ago, and that was because I couldn't say no to her. Plus Will and Kate swam around a glass bowl, required a few fish flakes a day, and were happy with their lot. Cats needed feeding and petting, they needed vets. Vets cost money.

"Can't you drop her at the shelter?"

He shook his head. "I have the pack social to organize."

I rolled my eyes. "Fine, I'll take her." The White Furry Menace hissed at me. I arched an eyebrow. Or maybe not.

"Good luck with that," Dave chuckled. "You'll let me know the outcome?"

Grabbing my copper hair, I piled it on top of my head and snapped a band around it, then knocked the tap on and began scrubbing my hands. The dead might not catch diseases, but they still deserved our respect. "Sure, any details since we last spoke?"

"Daniel Murray. He was found in a rented trailer on the outskirts of town. Joan, the owner, went to retrieve the rent this morning and found his door wide open and him dead on the floor. She called the pack in a panic. He was a recluse, so unlikely to be a fight. Plus, his face is weird."

I frowned as I dried my hands on a paper towel and snapped on a pair of gloves. "Weird how?"

Dave waved his hand at the bag. "You'll see."

Coming toe to toe with the White Furry Menace, who stared at my toes in my sandals like they were delicious mice, I unzipped the bag and blinked. Daniel Murray stared at the plain ceiling with milky eyes. That wasn't the unusual part. It was his mouth fixed in a permanent scream position with a look of pure terror plastered across his face. That wasn't normal. His arm twitched, Dangerous Dave jumped.

"It's an involuntary muscle spasm," I explained to the hard assed shifter.

"It's weird, Cora."

I rolled my eyes and glanced down at the white menace. "Tough guy, huh?"

She blinked at me in sister solidarity. Dave cleared his throat. "Why am I not surprised The Undertaker is more comfortable talking to animals than humans?"

I blinked at him and waited for the irony to sink into his thick skull. "This from the male who sprouts fur on weekends and communicates through growls, snorts and snarls whilst howling at the moon and sniffing female butts as a way of saying 'I like you.'"

"I don't howl at the moon, Cora, stop stereotyping."

I snorted a laugh. I wonder if he knows the enigmatic asshole from the other night? Dave seemed like the type to know everyone. He folded his arms and flattened his lips. I glanced down at Daniel; what story was he about to tell me? I glanced up and found his chocolate brown eyes studying me. "I won't start until you leave," I told him.

He scowled, his brain trying to put the random pieces of information he knew about me together. This is the reason he was dangerous - he wanted to know everything. No stone or person in this case left unturned. The man was like a dog with a bone, or wolf in this instance. One day his patience would run out and he would come seeking my secrets. Whilst my retro psychic skills weren't illegal—they *were* unusual. As for talking to the dead - that was a major no, no matter your species. And the big secret? Nobody could know. The day Dangerous Dave's patience ran out, would be the day he would either be disappointed or dead. I hoped it was the former.

"Fine. I have too much pack shit to sort out, anyway."

"Good luck with that," I said, chasing Dave out the door. He glanced at Daniel, then let the metal door go. I slammed the bar across, sealing myself in the room with the dead guy and the White Furry Menace. This is where I became the most vulnerable. But she could stay. It was her owner I was here to analyze, the least I could do was let her observe; as far as I was aware, cats couldn't tell my secrets.

I wheeled around the small cart of tools I used for this purpose, selected a sharp pair of scissors and began cutting Daniel's clothes from his stiff body. His auburn hair was absent of grey, suggesting he wasn't past midlife for a shifter. He'd been deceased awhile, from his eyes and rigor mortis I would guess around eight hours. The clothes fell away from the body in neat strips, which I placed in a zip-lock bag. Not once had Dave asked me for evidence, but then again the bodies he sent my way were for me to confirm his suspicions, and so far he had a one hundred percent guess rate. I frowned at the sealed door. This was the first time he hadn't told me what he expected me to find. It was probably the stress of the pack social.

I glanced at Daniel's expression and then examined his body one section at a time. There were no wounds, which was a good thing for me. I liked to prepare myself for what was coming. An examination of his nails and hands found no evidence of a struggle. Daniel looked on the outside like he just dropped dead; except shifters didn't just drop dead at Daniel's age, which made the next part more than a little nerve racking.

I pulled off my gloves, laid them on the tray and rolled the cart to the far left wall. I glanced at the White Furry Menace who was sitting with her perky tail straight up in the air like a regal queen. Great, I'd been lumbered with feline royalty. She could join Rebecca - they'd be good company for each other. She rumbled a soft purr at my stare, reminding me to get on with the part of my job which might take an hour from my life, or five depending on the severity.

I took a deep breath, stepped up to Daniel and grasped his hand. My world slid into black and then came into focus

55

as I found myself inside the tiny kitchenette area of a trailer. Scattered beer cans littered the worktop and the threadbare burgundy carpet. Yellowed net curtains framed the windows, and the stench of smoke clung to every molecule. Anxiety bit at my nerves as my gaze swung to the shadow crawling along the otherwise sunlit floor. I took a step back, knocking over some empty beer cans. My breath became more labored and my hand flew to my chest to rub the tightening ache expanding from the center. My eyes skittered around, searching for help. A weapon, salvation. Anything. It felt like a balloon was being expanded in my chest. Sweat rolled down my back and nausea churned in my gut. The shadow rose from the floor and took form in front of me. The piercing pain in my chest buckled my knees as the shadow's eyes burned with pits of fire. Its mouth split into a wide grin as it seemed to look past Daniel and straight into my soul. Impossible, my brain shoved in front. This was the past. The pain built into a never ending crescendo and my heated blood swished in my ears like waves of death, holding me in its grip and pulling me away from the mortal plane. My mouth opened wide in a silent scream as I tried to pull away from the moment of death, my psyche too wrapped up in what was happening for me to separate out past and present. Daniel died terrified and in excruciating pain.

I was being tickled by something wet, soft and insistent on my fingertips. My head pounded on the left, and I was on a hard cool surface which made my back ache. I blinked my eyes open to come face to face with the White Furry Menace; she gave me a haughty stare and sat on her haunches to preen her belly. Guess my fingertips weren't yummy. I glanced up to find Daniel's arm hanging at an odd angle. Well this was new, whilst weak I could normally get to the chaise longue in my office next door before passing out. I groaned as I rolled onto my side, a sharp pain echoed through my chest in reminder of what I'd experienced through Daniel's eyes. He'd died of a heart attack, except shifters didn't have heart attacks. No, he died from an induced heart attack caused by... my mind scrambled for the cause. There was a shadow, fire, and then pain. How was I going to explain that?

I groaned. Dave would scrutinize every detail. I rolled to my stomach and pushed up, my arms gave out and the lab swayed. Nope, crawling it was. The White Furry Menace looked on, unimpressed with my slow crawl towards the door which linked to the office. I paused halfway and sank to the floor, a mess of shaky limbs and sweaty palms. The White Furry Menace blinked. "I'd like to see you do better on two," I mumbled.

It took agonizing minutes to reach the door, and twice as long to twist the internal lock before I spilled into the office and made it to the soft chaise longue. I dragged the quilt over my body as the shivers crept in. Oh boy, this recovery was going to be a doozy. I dragged my phone out of my shorts, realizing I'd lost almost two hours on the floor. The White Furry Menace shot onto the quilt, kneaded my thighs and settled on my lap like I was her personal cushion. Before I gave into exhaustion, I hit the SOS message to Rebecca; I patted the cat's head. She was like velvet. "Food and functional adults will be here soon," I muttered.

"Cora?" Rebecca's melodic voice sing-songed through my hazy dream.

"Why is she trembling this bad?" A gruff voice asked. Oh no. I could count on one hand the people who had seen me in this state, and Dave wasn't one of them. Yes, he knew I got cravings for food and needed fuel for some of what I did.

"She must have taken a hit with the body you left her." Too much information Rebecca, shut up.

I peeled my mouth open, my lips sticking together. She shoved a straw in between them. "Drink, Cora."

"This is what it does to her to figure out the cause of death?" Dave said, his voice clinical. He was dissecting this with the precision of a surgeon.

"Not always, it depends on the cause," Rebecca replied. Vampires, world's biggest gossips; shifters, world's biggest secret hoarders. And lucky me, I have both discussing my secrets over my incapacitated body.

"So the cause determines her reaction?" Dave asked.

"Erm… I'm not sure what determines her reaction. Violence, I think."

"Cora?" Dave said.

My eyes split open, noting the shadows shrouding the room. Sunlight had given way to the moon. Wow, I'd really been out of it. I'd never had that happen from a retro session before. Dave smiled, which was less than reassuring. "Can you sit up?" he asked, already shoving his hands under my arms. The White Furry Menace shot off my lap and into the main house somewhere.

I heaved a breath, glorying in the painless motion. "What time is it?" I croaked.

Dave frowned. "About ten."

I nodded, already making a mental list of all the patients I'd been due to see today. Only two needed urgent follow-up visits. I could manage that.

I swung my legs over the side of the makeshift bed, my aunt's quilt slipping to the floor. I used my unsteadiness as a cover to find the right words for Dave. He would want an explanation, and I was scrambling for one that made sense.

"What happened?" he asked, grabbing a guest chair and pulling it in front of me. I hated being interrogated, I hated being interrogated in my home even more.

"Daniel died of a heart attack," I stated before guzzling down the rest of the juice. Rebecca placed another one in my hand and then made herself scarce. It's not like she couldn't hear the conversation no matter where she was in the house, but this gave us the illusion of privacy.

Dave frowned and grasped his hands together in front of him, leaning towards me. "Shifters don't have heart attacks."

"I'm aware, but this one did."

"Did you do an autopsy?"

I shook my head. "No, I can if you want me to verify it. But the pain I felt, the pain Daniel felt—it was a classic heart attack."

He leaned back, his chocolate brown eyes boring into my soul and seeking my secrets. "This is why you lock yourself in the lab. You are vulnerable."

The sugar burns through my haziness, and my limbs settle. "Why are you here?" I asked, tilting my head.

He lifted his phone and flipped it around, showing me the SOS message. "You texted me."

I hit the last number instead of Rebecca. Oh boy, my mistakes were going to cost me if this led to the pack's head honcho making my business his business.

"Sorry, I meant it for Rebecca."

He nodded. "That much I got when Rebecca flew into a panic."

"It's because he died of a heart attack. They don't normally take that much from me."

He sighed and looked at the floor, his hands clenched together. "Shifters don't have heart attacks, and if they did, it's unlikely they would die from it."

"This one did, and there was something in the trailer with him."

"Something?"

I blew out a heavy breath. "A shadow which morphed into a being. I'm pretty sure that influenced whatever medical thing happened to Daniel."

Dave tilted his head. His eyebrows snapped together. "You're a retro." I nodded. Don't dig too far, Dave. "You can see the ultimate moments before someone's death, but only after the fact."

"Yes," I whispered.

He ran a hand through his dark wavy hair. The strands bouncing back into place. "I'll keep your secret, Cora. But I need your help."

My head snapped up to see if he was serious. "Why?"

His eyes tightened. "I need you to look into pack deaths as well as loners."

"It's been happening in the pack?"

He shrugged. "There have been a couple of unusual deaths. I don't like unknowns or loose ends. In the past two weeks, I've had to bury two pack members with no obvious cause of death. They happen from time to time, but two, and now this loner."

"You think they are linked?"

He tilts his head. "I would be a fool to ignore the possibility, and a bigger fool to not employ the most qualified person in the region to look into them."

Silence stretched between us like an elastic band. I had no reason to say no, except he needed me more than I needed him right now.

"What do you want?" he asked.

Hmm, good question. Squeezing my reasonable price up might damage the relationship between me and Dave. I needed the business, and he could easily stop looking at loner deaths.

"A favor," I responded.

His eyes narrowed. "From me?"

I shook my head. "No."

His jaw ticked. "You want a pack favor?"

"Yes."

"What?"

I shook my head. "I don't know yet. When the time comes, I want a favor from the pack." I held my breath as I waited for his decision. At the end of the day, I would do the work, I needed the money. But pack favors were both rare and powerful. They held a lot of sway in North America and were the holy grail of prizes in the pack.

He held his hand out. "Deal."

CHAPTER SIX

Piss a man off and expect retribution, piss a woman off and expect a reckoning.

I pushed Dangerous Dave out the lab door with promises of updates should any further loners meet an untimely and unnatural death this evening. He left looking harassed and distracted. The shifter deaths and the pack social he was late for, on his mind.

I dragged my heavy legs up the stairs to the main floor, hoping that at - I glanced at my watch - ten thirty-two pm, all the residents of Summer Grove were tucked up in their beds or at least too tired to warrant more than a passing greeting. Rebecca lounged on the reception desk like a priceless sculpture and Maggie sat on the chair, both their eyes trained on me as I ascended the last step. Rolling my eyes required effort I couldn't muster. Both shifter and vampire would have heard that discussion, so the questions burning in their eyes would no doubt come tumbling my way. I'd long since given up hope of privacy.

"What?" I asked as I shuffled towards them. My temple pounded, warning me I needed more sleep and a cookie or two.

"You garnered a favor from the pack," Rebecca stated.

"From Dangerous Dave," Maggie added, her eyes extra wide.

"They require my services, and nobody within a five hundred-mile radius can perform a retro read. So I took advantage of the situation."

"You could have asked for more money," Rebecca pointed out.

"We'll have more money coming in if I am reviewing every shifter death."

Rebecca nodded. For all the blonde hair, she was far from a bimbo; she was a trained royal political strategist in hiding. "You need fuel before you go upstairs," Rebecca pointed out. With her vampire hearing I couldn't hide the fact I spoke to the dead. She occupied the room under mine, so it was the truth, or I let her believe I was a few currants short of a fruitcake. The pair slid from their perches and flanked me as we made our way to the kitchen. The smell of warm peach pie drifting down the hallway made my mouth water and my legs pick up speed.

I rounded the corner, sank onto the bench, and shoveled the first forkful of pie straight from the dish. Rebecca chuckled as she grabbed a fork and slid a dainty piece into her mouth. Maggie sat next to me and wrinkled her nose. Fruit anything wasn't her forte. I ate with the manners of a starved man as I sucked in cool air to manage the too hot pie.

"So, a shadow?" Rebecca asked after I'd eaten half the pie and the pounding in my temple was an echo in the background. Sleep was next on the agenda, the restful kind, not the knocked out cold kind.

"A shadow," I confirmed, "with eyes like a demon."

Rebecca frowned. "Demons aren't real."

"I know."

"So they made it to look like a demon, which means…"

"Magic, an elemental."

Maggie dropped her chin into her hand and glanced between us. "So why would Dangerous Dave trust Cora?"

I snorted a laugh. "Dave trusts no one. But if he wants someone to experience with clarity what happened to these shifters, I'm your girl."

A loud bang blurred through my mind, almost knocking my ass off the bench and onto the floor. It happened again, I winced. Rebecca frowned. "What's up?"

"Boundary wards, someone is trying to breach them."

She shot out of her seat and flew out of the kitchen at vampire speed; the fork clattering to the floor after she disappeared. Vampire fact: they were crazy fast.

Maggie's eyes widened as she glanced around. I patted her hand. She couldn't hear or feel the wards. I'd tied them to the house, and the house was tied to my magic. It would deny entry to anyone or anything trying to get past the property boundary who meant me or my residents harm. I had built in a warning system two years ago, which meant the physical push from the wards manifested in my mind. I could be anywhere on the planet and know if the house was under attack.

"I'm sure it's just some wolves or other wildlife hunting," I reassured her. Her hand trembled under mine, a product of being terrified of your own family and friends. I could relate. "Stay here."

I slid from my seat and clambered after the speedy vampire. Rebecca might be in hiding, but she was fierce about protecting her hideout and me. She was no shrinking violet. If someone was trying to hurt me or the house, we would meet them with a bloody, swift and violent end.

The front door lay open. The sweltering night air swept through the house, seeking and obliterating the cool shadows. Perhaps I could afford to fix the air conditioning on the main floor if I had enough extra work. It sounded as if I was wishing more shifters dead; I wasn't, and it wasn't like I was out murdering them for financial gain. If I went illegal, there were far more lucrative ventures. Did you know the human body is worth over $450,000 on the black market? I'd never do anything so deplorable. I was serious when I took my oath to do no harm. I grabbed the shotgun from the umbrella basket at the entrance and stepped out onto the porch. Rebecca's features had sharpened, her cheekbones looked like they could cut glass. Whatever was out here had spooked her vampire side enough to make itself known. Her eyes glistened silver as she glanced at me, then went back to studying the ominous outskirts of the property. "What's out there?" I asked her.

A shiver of magic skimmed my flesh, goosebumps popped up over my legs and arms. "Something unnatural," she whispered. Eyesight sharper than any sniper rifle was also another bonus vampires shared with shifters.

"It set off the ward boundaries which means it means us harm."

Her head twitched to the right. "There, under the first arching oak."

I narrowed my eyes and waited for whatever she could see to make itself known. "Where?" I murmured after a solid minute.

A figure clad in a black cloak darted underneath the draping branches of the oak, moving along the boundary. "See it?" she whispered.

I nodded and loaded the shotgun. A warning shot would deter most people. Here's hoping this was your average human. I narrowed my eyes as the cloak shifted in an unfelt breeze. The night air was as still as the vampire next to me, cluing me in that this visitor wasn't human.

I hiked the shotgun up and aimed at the last place I'd seen the cloak. The bang echoed through the property. The trees rustled as the less predatory wildlife fled. The cloak didn't move. I squinted, it was there, an unnatural presence in my otherwise peaceful oasis.

"You missed," Rebecca said.

"I didn't want to hit the trees."

She smothered a laugh. "The trees will forgive you if you protect the property from whatever the hell that is."

"You are trespassing on private property. Remove yourself now." No response. I took aim and fired. The figure moved fast, zipping across the lawn towards us. The pain of the ward breach brought me to my knees, the gun clattering to the floorboards on the porch. Rebecca sank with me, her hands under my arms as she dragged me backwards with speed. The figure closed in on the steps leading up to the porch, stopping mere feet from the ward. Tendrils of power snaked out from him, slithering through the ward with ease and snapped around my ankles, jerking me to a stop.

Rebecca fell on her backside. I yelped as I became the rope in a supernatural tug of war. "Rebecca," I cried out.

"I know," she mumbled. The cloaked figure yanked again. I slid an inch towards him. Rebecca wrapped her legs around my waist and locked her ankles. "Ready?" she asked.

Rebecca tugged, and I slammed my hand out, reinforcing the secondary wards surrounding the house. The tendrils slithered off me as the figure howled in rage. Rebecca crawled backwards and flung the door shut with her foot just as the cloaked figure hit the bottom step. An unholy screech sounded as they hit the ward and tried to force their way through. A scream was ripped from my throat as my hands slammed over my ears. Rebecca dropped me with a thud. I twisted to find her passed out on the floor. I glanced further into the house to find Maggie slumped against the wall, her eyes closed. What the hell just happened?

I spun onto my stomach and crawled towards Rebecca as the thing outside continued to screech as it hit the wards again and again. Agony whipping through me with each strike like lightning. When something came to claim your life, you provided the biggest deterrent you had. Pain was an excellent tool. However, this maniac, whilst pissed, continued to test the house boundary. I pressed my fingers to Rebecca's throat, feeling her heartbeat, strong and sure. My legs wobbled as I climbed to my feet and stumbled to a paling Maggie. I checked her pulse. They were both passed out, either from the ward's magic or from the thing trying to gain entry. Nothing had ever bothered trying to get past the boundary wards before, let alone try to get further before today. Whatever it was, it wanted to harm someone in here. A sweeping silence coated the house. That terrified me more than the booming, crazy assed psycho trying to get in. Loud, I could track. Silent and deadly, I wouldn't see coming, and my supernatural eyes and ears were out for the count on the floor.

I crept to the window and moved the curtain. I scanned the night. Someone was out there, but they were regrouping, assessing and plotting. Their initial attack had been unsuccessful and now they were planning a different route, an alternative method of entry. What's the probability that I relive a shifter heart attack and then come under attack on the same day? I was a numbers girl, and whilst coincidences happened, they didn't happen to this degree. No, whatever was out there was linked to Daniel. Shit.

I spun on my heel and took the stairs down to the lab two at a time, no easy feat with my legs. I burst through the door, finding Daniel where I'd left him but with the White Furry Menace sitting on his chest. She hissed at me. Trust me to get stuck with a feline that had the sparkling personality one would expect from a shark.

I glanced around the quiet room. The external door remained barred and intact. Maybe the thing outside didn't know where I kept my bodies. I did a quick scan of my office and then raced back upstairs. Rebecca sat up shaking her head. Her amber eyes met mine.

"It's gone?" she asked.

"I think so."

"I can't feel its magic."

"Me neither," I confirmed.

Rebecca looked behind me to Maggie's slumped form. "It knocked us all out?"

"Everyone but me, I think it was the ward."

She frowned and tilted her head. "Okay, maybe."

An animalistic growl froze us both. The White Furry Menace prowled towards us, her hackles raised. She slinked past us. Rebecca and I watched in shock as the feline leapt onto the windowsill and disappeared behind the curtain. She hissed and made general unhappy sounds at the night.

"Are we sure it's gone?" I wondered.

The White Furry Menace dropped to the floor with a hefty thud and strolled past us with a haughty look, like she had single-handedly dispatched the creature crawling in the night.

"Does she have a name?" Rebecca asked.

"Not yet, I've just gone with the White Furry Menace." The feline stuck her tail in the air, ensuring we got a good look at her backside. Rebecca and I looked at each other.

"I like her," Rebecca said.

"She's a beautiful female with a slinky walk and an attitude, of course you do." The cat in question paused and eyeballed Will and Kate swimming in the glass bowl. I pointed at her. "You will not eat my goldfish."

She glanced at me over her shoulder, then trotted off into the house. Apparently goldfish are beneath her.

CHAPTER SEVEN

My knights come bearing burgers. Haughty lords with

jewels need not apply.

I made it to my rooms with no more surprises. One last task, then I could sleep. Oh beautiful, glorious sleep. My first client was at eleven am; Rebecca had rearranged my appointments from today which still gave me a decent stretch of snooze time. I shoved the door open and closed it quietly, not wanting to disturb any guests with supernatural hearing. Daniel stood in the middle of my living room between the two sofas, spinning around slowly. He would have had enough time to figure some shit out by now, which meant this should be short and sweet.

He glanced up and strode towards me, sticking out his hand. "Good evening, my name is Daniel, I seem to have lost my way."

Oh boy. I ignored his hand and went to my sink. I found most ghosts kept the kitchen island between us, Daniel was no different, giving me the distance I needed to inform him of his untimely demise and afterlife outlook. But first I needed to see what he could remember. Right now, his subconscious was blocking the fact that he was dead. This happened about fifty percent of the time, which meant I had to ease the dead into realizing they weren't meeting their best friend in the local bar like every night, unless they too were dead and they had bars in heaven. Huh, what did they have in heaven?

"I'm Cora," I informed him. "And you are dead."

He blinked. Subtlety was not my strong point, I never claimed to have the best bedside manner. I had emotions, but processing other people's was draining.

"I beg your pardon," he stated, attempting to pull his shirt down over his pouch belly.

"Daniel, you died early this morning in your trailer."

He stumbled back... straight through the sofa and stopped inside the coffee table. He glanced down to find his feet hidden by the heavy oak plane.

"I'm dead?" he whispered.

I filled the kettle and popped it on the stove. A nice cup of chamomile ought to do the trick. "Do you remember being in your trailer this morning?"

"I... well... yes, I think... no."

I focused on the memory and tried to pick out something to help. "You read the White Castle Chronicle?" I said, remembering the paper on the sofa.

He frowned. "Yes."

"Yesterday's headline was the market owner's costly stalls? It's putting off new market stalls and driving the old ones away?"

He rubbed a hand over his face and looked around my room again. "Yes I remember, then I went to make a coffee."

"What else do you remember?"

"Cold, I was so cold." He shivers a little, then clutches his chest. Here it comes. "Pain, the pain in my chest. I think I

78

had a heart attack, but shifters don't have heart attacks, otherwise I'd lay off Ruby's pancakes and bacon."

"Do you remember anyone in the trailer?"

He shook his head. "No, I was alone." Huh, maybe he couldn't remember.

"You sure?"

He nodded. "I'm dead? Like no heart beating, cold hard in the ground dead?"

I winced. "You haven't been buried yet."

His eyes locked with mine. "What? Where am I?"

"In my lab…"

He blinks out of existence. The dead for some unfathomable reason could always seek out their own bodies, but when they found them the results were never good. The kettle whistles behind me as I wonder why he hadn't been able to see the shadow in his room. I could see it, and I was only reliving Daniel's last moments through his eyes. He must be blocking it. I drop the tea bag in the mug and douse it in hot liquid. Daniel reappears less than a foot from me. His face is pale and tiny beads of sweat shine on his forehead. The physiological responses in the dead seemed to be similar to the living. Which, given they no longer had a pulse, was odd. Who was I to question the Almighty's logic?

"I'm dead," he whispered.

I folded my arms and leaned back against the sink. "You are."

"Where will I be buried? I have no family or mate."

"I can bury you in a plot on my land, there is space underneath a giant magnolia."

He frowned. "You would do that for me?"

"I will, but it's not true shifter consecrated ground. I can offer you peace, but not the afterlife you would have on pack grounds."

He nodded. "I would like that very much, thank you…" He'd forgotten my name already.

"Cora."

He smiled. "Thank you, Cora."

"Come with me," I said, leading him towards the locked door and through to the little peace I could offer a lost soul.

"The bone has set and healed in the correct position," I informed Mrs. Fleming. She glanced at her toddler son bouncing around my office with the wild abandon commonly seen in child shifters. He was seeking his next disaster, now that he'd won his fight with gravity out of his bedroom window. Fox shifter toddlers were notoriously boisterous. She had her hands full with a toddler and a male teenager who had recently discovered the allure of the opposite sex. A wistful part of me mourned for the kids I was unlikely to bear. For elementals, permanent joining meant sharing your power. But the union was sexist. The power exchange went one way, from female to male. There was an entire department of PhD people stored away in the archives of the Order, devoted to demystifying these quirks of nature. So far their collective neurons had theorized that in the time of the male being the protector and provider he would need the power if facing off with say, a mammoth or sabre-tooth tiger. But the genetic trade hadn't yet caught up to the present, and as such unions were rare. My mother fell hard for my father. They kept their union a secret for many reasons, and before anybody knew, she was six months pregnant and glowing. My grandmother disapproved of the union. When my father was forced to return to his homeland, my mother became heartbroken and depressed. She was such an aloof figure that when she took her own life, I approached it with the detached manner of an acquaintance, sad they were gone, but in reality it impacted little on my day-to-day life. I spent more time bouncing around my aunts than at home. I was even schooled in Louisiana rather than New York, where I'm originally from.

"Thank you, Doctor Cora," Mrs. Fleming said, chasing the toddler terror away from chewing on my potted plants.

I ushered the duo out of the door and up the stairs. "You're welcome." Maggie gave the little guy a wave. He winked at her. I closed the front door after them with a thud and leaned against it. Doubling up on clients to catch up on yesterday had taken its toll on me. I glanced at the grandfather clock, nine at night.

"I made pot roast," Maggie chirped.

I nodded and strolled to the kitchen, my taste buds already reorganizing their defenses against whatever pot roast was Maggie style. Rebecca sat at the table with a small smile on her lips as she painted her nails coral to match her sheath dress. A plate rested in the center of the table, empty but for a few brown crumbs. I frowned.

"What happened to the pot roast?" I asked.

Rebecca dipped the brush in the bottle and glanced at me. "The Allison's and the Herbert's were hungry. I couldn't say no—guests first, right?"

Maggie parks her hands on her hips. "I made that for you," she pouted.

I waved her off. "It's fine, a sandwich will do."

"No need, the cavalry is on the way," Rebecca said with a wink.

What the hell was she planning now? I rubbed the back of my neck and glared at her. "Cavalry?"

The front door opened with its customary creak and the slap of Italian loafers against my wooden floor declared the arrival of my cavalry. Sebastian Elliot rounded the corner, a brown paper takeout bag in hand. Sebastian was the devil in Armani. He was beautiful in a way that made you squint to find the flaws. There weren't any. The Vampire Prince of North America was perfection personified. Nordic blue eyes like ice chips and long silky raven hair. I liked my men with flaws, calloused hands, not ones that were as soft as velvet.

But appearances in this case were deceiving, as Sebastian was one of the most ruthless and capable people I knew.

"I come bearing burgers," his voice slid around the room like silk as he waggled the bag in front of me.

"You're a god," I mumbled, grabbing the bag from him and sliding out the four burgers and accompanying fries onto the empty pot roast plate.

Rebecca wrinkled her nose. "Yeah, the burger god," she mumbled.

I unwrapped the burger and sank my teeth into it. Sebastian slid onto the seat next to me and picked up a few fries. "You're early," I pointed out.

"You need fuel before we train," he said, chomping on the fries.

Maggie plonked herself opposite Sebastian and grabbed a burger. Seems our budding chef was also hungry. "True," I replied. "But you are two hours early."

He shrugged. "I have other commitments later tonight."

I arched an eyebrow. He flicked a look at the shifter and vampire opposite us. Fine, he could keep his secrets—until later, anyway. "What's happening in vampire upper society?"

His lips twitched. "Collecting secrets?"

I shook my head as I unwrapped burger number two. "Nope, but it's like listening to 'Pride and Prejudice' with a bloodthirsty twist."

The vampires were ruled by a royal family in each territory, and just like elementals, they revered blood lines. Vampires were the snobs of the supernatural world, whilst the Principal - the strongest, most feared leader - ruled the shifters.

The vampires reveled in politics, both their own and that of the human world. They spent an abnormal amount of time analyzing other vampire houses' actions. Why they did something, what that means, and how can they benefit from it. Whilst the shifters rejected other factions' problems, unless the problem strayed into their territory or one of their own was involved. Then the entire pack moved to resolve the problem, violently, without remorse and without regret. Elementals remained aloof and above reproach. We were the most separate, other factions considered our abilities unnatural despite our power being drawn from the elements surrounding us.

"House Greenberg has sired another heir, making that their tenth—yet a male heir remains elusive." Myth: A vampire bite results in a new vampire. Reality: if a vampire bit you, it was for nutritional purposes. Shifters, like vampires, were a different species. Biting resulted in blood loss, and nothing more. Both species grew in numbers by the traditional method of procreation.

Rebecca chuckled. "Ten women, Margaret will have her hands full."

"What else?" I asked, swiping a salty fry from the plate.

"Mother and father have impressed on me the importance of finding a suitable match before my seventieth year."

"We have six years to find you a suitable bride."

He nodded. "In the meantime, I am to still continue the monthly commitment to bring before them a suitable candidate once a month."

I threw my head back and groaned. "It can't be that time of the month already."

The three of them chuckled. I glared at Maggie and Rebecca. Traitors. Rebecca's lips tilted up. "What? I like to see you in a gown once a month. You have fabulous curves for such a short woman."

I rolled my eyes. "Fine, when?"

"This Saturday," Sebastian answered.

I stood and grabbed the wrappers, depositing them in the bin, the burgers and fries demolished.

"Right well, barring death by misadventure, I'll be there. Midnight?" I checked.

Sebastian stood, his movements liquid and graceful. "As always."

"Your mother does have a flair for the dramatic," I said, stepping out of the kitchen, trudging down the hallway and descending the stairs, my vampire best friend at my back.

"You training like that?" he asked as I turned down the hallway in the opposite direction from my office and lab. I glanced down at my slacks and T-shirt and shrugged.

"An attacker won't wait for me to get changed into more comfortable clothes."

My palm hit the plain white door, and we stepped into a large makeshift dojo. Black mats dotted the wooden floor, shielding me from the worst of the bruises each session cost me. Sebastian opened a wooden chest next to the door and selected two twelve-inch knives.

"Knife training, you know how to treat a girl," I said, bouncing on my toes.

He placed the knives on the top of the chest, whipped his suit jacket off and folded it on top. Then he tied his hair back in a neat knot. He grabbed the knives and spun them around in each palm, the dexterity of the movement too fluid to be human.

"No knives for you," he said, a wicked gleam in his eyes. Every week he changed the pace, altered the parameters, introduced new moves. The training kept me on my toes and bolstered my confidence at being able to defend myself in situations people should never find themselves in. It also tested the chains I kept locked tight against my true form. When I was under stress or in pain, my true form strained against the shackles I'd wrapped myself in. They could never break.

I braced my feet apart and tracked his movements. He telegraphed his move like a typical attacker, but Sebastian was far from typical, and I had learnt over the years to expect the unexpected. He moved left, inserting a little vampire speed.

His hand shot out, I stepped to the left, spun one hundred and eighty degrees into his chest and knocked his knife wielding arm to the side.

He brought his other hand towards my throat, the wicked knife gleaming.

I spun under his arm, grabbed his wrist and twisted it behind his back.

My foot connected with the back of his knees and he went down to the floor with a thud. I sprawled on his back and shoved my knee against his side, locking one arm in place under him, whilst my hands kept his wrist secure.

My thumb dug into the pressure point on his hand, and he released the knife with a chuckle. "Excellent," he drawled.

I pushed off him, and he leapt to his feet. He spun to face me and threw a knife; I dodged to the right as it sailed past me and embedded itself in the plain white wall, making another mark to join the many others. These I didn't fill. I considered each one a minor victory.

He nodded like a pleased sensei, then threw the other knife at the wall—this time not aiming for me. He sunk into a fighting stance, assessed me in a split second, then moved with a swiftness reserved for the supernaturally inclined. I saw his hand coming towards my solar plexus and leaned back to mitigate the blow.

Sebastian rule number fifteen: if you can't avoid the blow, minimize it. The air huffed out of my chest and I winced at the sharp pain. Instead of curling in on myself, I threw my hand up and slammed my palm into his chin. His neck cracked as his head snapped back. A lesser being would have crumpled in pain. Sebastian grunted, then grinned.

"Good shot," he mumbled. I didn't return his smile, and I didn't take my eyes off him. At the beginning I'd basked in his praise, and every time he taught me a hard lesson on why you never drop your guard around a predator. "Okay, fifty circuits. Then we go again."

I relaxed my muscles and began circling the room at a steady pace. He sat in the middle of the room cross legged with his shirt sleeves rolled up, randomly shouting out instructions. "Duck, jump, roll." A knife or two whistled my way every so often.

Half way through my laps a light sheen of sweat coated my skin and I reconsidered my decision to not change. "What has you so distracted?" Sebastian asks.

I arched an eyebrow as I ran behind his back. "What makes you think I'm distracted?"

"I gave you twice the amount of cardio, and you didn't bitch me out."

"I don't bitch." He tilted his head. I slid to a stop and collapsed in front of him. "Dave had me read a lone shifter yesterday."

"Okay, not unusual."

"Not until I got his death memory," I rubbed the back of my neck. "He died of a heart attack."

"Huh," he said. "That is unusual."

I nodded. "There was something in the room with him. I think it caused the heart attack. It wasn't natural."

"How much time out did that cost you?"

"A few hours initially, then many more later on."

He sucked his lips against his teeth. "What was in the room?"

"A shadow with eyes like fire."

He blinked. "So magic? An elemental killed a shifter?"

I shrugged and picked at a wrinkle in my slacks. "Dave didn't leap to that conclusion."

Sebastian shook his head. "Why on earth would you supply Dangerous Dave with information against your own kind?"

I squinted at him. "I told him the truth."

His stare hardened. "You told him you are retro."

"He figured it out, he won't tell anyone."

His hand slammed against the mat. "You better hope he tells no one. The last time you trusted someone…"

A phantom sharp pain blazed across my abdomen in remembrance. I rubbed the area. The chains stretched in anticipation of fighting a foe long since thwarted. I rolled my shoulders to shake it off. "He won't."

He glanced at my hand, his eyes tightening in a shared memory. "Good, because whilst you have your little wards set up around this house, that won't stop idiots from trying to snatch you from the store or the gas station should they learn of your abilities."

"And misunderstand them," I finished, blinking back tears. Retros were so rare, that when people learnt of your ability to read past events, they assumed future ones were also a given. They weren't. I would never again live in the fear that had consumed me from the inside out. If someone wanted to come at me for my gift, then they would face a capable, strong elemental, not the feeble little girl I had once been. "This is why we train," I pointed out.

He ran a hand over his head and pulled the hair tie out. "We train to give you a better chance, you aren't invincible, Cora, never think that." Sebastian's rule number six, there's always someone stronger, faster, smarter, more prepared than you.

I huffed out a breath and tucked a strand of wayward copper hair back into my ponytail. "Dave asked me to look into all shifter deaths from this point forward, including pack ones."

"All deaths? Have there been many?"

I rolled my eyes. Sebastian, the Vampire Prince of North America, was assessing what this meant for his faction. "This is not about politics, this is about me having the funds to fix the air conditioning."

"Everything is about politics. Why would he have you look into pack deaths unless they had unexplained ones?"

I shrugged. "Not sure, but there's something else." Nordic blue eyes assessed me with a gaze sharp enough to cut diamond. "Last night the perimeter ward was breached and something tried to get in the house."

Silence stretched in the room. Never try to out wait a vampire. They had a far longer life span to sit in

93

uncomfortable silence. I huffed. "It looked suspiciously like the thing that was in the room with the loner."

"And it got past the perimeter wards?" I nodded. Sebastian frowned. "Was it after the shifter body or you?"

"Body, I think. There is no reason for it to be after me."

"Politics," he reminded me. Well, yes, politics might mean some elemental foe had sent a creature that looked like it had climbed out of the depths of hell to my door. But again, for what purpose? "Have you informed the Order?"

I scoffed. "I'm not a fool, I need to keep the Order and the crazy assed bitch away from me and my life as much as possible."

"But if it turns out to be an elemental?"

"Then I will be asking for forgiveness rather than permission."

He nodded. "So you agreed to look into the pack's deaths?"

"Yes, for extra money and a pack favor."

He smirked. "Clever girl. We'll make a leader out of you yet."

We stood, and he collected his jacket, throwing it on. Not a bead of sweat from our workout. Damn vampires and their lack of perspiration. I pulled open the door and the White Furry Menace shot through my legs and came to a halt in front of Sebastian. She dropped a small furry brown blob at his feet and slapped her left paw on its back. It squeaked and struggled. He tilted his head; she tilted hers to match. A slow smile crept across his face. She slinked her way around his legs. He didn't even bitch about the white hairs on his suit trousers.

"You have a cat," he stated.

I squinted at the creature she'd brought him. "No, I have a stowaway—she came in with the loner, and if I mention the word S-H-E-L-T-E-R, she-" The White Furry Menace hissed at me. "Does that. Can cats spell?"

"This one does," he said, leaning down and giving her a languid stroke. Keeping her paw on the mouse, she arched her back and purred.

I threw my hands in the air. "That's right, purr for the vampire who hasn't fed you and bring him gifts. But hiss at me."

CHAPTER EIGHT

Take me to your leader.

A shrill ring cut through my dream. The burning pits of fire and shadows slunk from my mind, their devious eyes promised further fitful-filled sleep in the future. My hand slapped the side of my bedside table. The wooden lamp wobbled, then gravity took it to the floor with a clunk. My fingers grasped the rectangular nuisance, and I swiped right with my thumb to accept the call.

"Are you awake?" Dave asked. A low rumble in the background suggested he was in a vehicle. I sat up, ran a hand through my hair and rubbed my eyes, forcing them open. Moonlight spilled through the window, casting a soft glow in my room. I glared at the oval mirror facing my bed and took in my bird's nest hair, skewed tank top and half-lidded eyes.

"No."

"I've got a body for you."

"You bring me such extraordinary gifts."

"It's one of our own, Cora. I need to know how and when." Less than twenty-four hours had passed, and I was already regretting my deal with the pack.

"Fine, drop them off at seven."

"Not good enough, I need information now."

I pulled the phone away from my ear. Two am, was he serious? "Now?" I checked.

"Now. I'll pay you an extra fifty."

"Double."

"Extra hundred." That was fifty percent, not double. I hung up, rolled over and dragged the soft cotton blanket over my head. The boundary wards gave a rude thud in my mind, letting me know I had a visitor. He wouldn't dare. Gravel crunched as a vehicle made its way to the house. The vehicle honked an urgent tune directly below my bedroom window. I groaned and threw back my covers. If Dave was this insistent at 2am, it had to be important.

I yanked my drawers open and slipped my legs into grey sleep shorts and my feet into sliders. I was out of my door and trotting down the stairs one minute later, a carton of apple juice in one hand and an energy bar in the other. Answers meant I would need my gift, and that required calories I didn't have to spare.

I stalked towards the lab door, an insistent banging letting me know Dave would not be taking no for an answer. I threw the bar to one side, and he yanked the door open. Dave looked me up and down.

I parked my hands on my hips. "If you want office dressed and ready Cora, you need to come during office hours."

Dave fisted his hands at his sides, his jaw set in a hard line. I frowned as two younger pack males unloaded a body wrapped in a pristine white sheet and waited for me to move. I stepped to the side and waved at the metal slab. They laid the body down and turned to Dave.

"Go home," he growled. A blonde male with startling blue eyes and full lips opened his mouth. "No," Dave said, cutting him off. "I will be back when I have answers, you can't do any more right now."

The blonde frowned at me, nodded, and then glanced over his shoulder at the white sheet before heading out and jumping in the black van. Dave's shoulders slumped as they peeled out of the garage. He shut and barred the door behind him.

"Can I stay?" he asked.

I shook my head. I'd known Dave for a few years, but that didn't make us friends or offer him the level of trust needed for him to be around when I used my gift. No one was allowed in the room whilst I performed a retro reading.

He nodded. "Can you at least keep the door unlocked?"

I glanced at the bright fluorescence on the ceiling. "Why?"

"I'd prefer you not be on the floor for hours again."

I blinked and met his stare. "No."

He lifted his hands and backed towards the office door. "Fine, I'll wait upstairs, but, Cora?"

"Yes?" I paused in the office door, having followed him to lock it.

"Hayley was one of our own, due to be mated to that boy next week."

"How old?" I asked.

"Twenty three," he stopped with his foot in the door. I raised an eyebrow. "There's something else you need to know."

"What?"

"She's small."

"Okay."

"With thick red hair." I stared at him, confused where this was going. "And green eyes."

I blinked. "Spit it out, Dave."

"She looks like you." With that bombshell, he spun on his heel, stalked through the office and disappeared up the stairs to the main floor. Wow, thanks, Dave.

I yanked the door closed, twisted the lock and spun towards the body. A shiver of warning worked its way up my spine. I crept closer, my hands shaking. I never felt uncomfortable around the dead. How could I when I could speak to them? I rolled my tray of tools over to the body, snapped on some blue plastic gloves and stood next to the white sheet.

"Get it together, Cora," I muttered and grabbed the scissors. I placed them at one end of the sheet, the blades poised open around delicate embroidery. They hadn't just wrapped her in any sheet, they'd put her in the best linen they could find. I slid the scissors back and dropped them on the tray. It took me a minute, but I found the end of the sheet and pulled it out from under her body, I let it fall to the side, her features more pronounced only being wrapped by one layer. I grabbed the opposite edge and tugged it out from under her body, throwing it to the other side.

My eyes stayed glued to her torso, the rabbit and fox print pajamas holding my attention whilst I built up the courage to look at her face. I drummed my fingers on the edge of the metal; the sound dulled by the sheet.

I darted my eyes up to her face, and my breath caught in my throat. She wasn't just a little like me. No, out of the thousands of possible victims, this girl could have been my sister—not quite a twin. Her nose was longer and her cheeks slimmer. I would say she was a touch more delicate than me. But the similarities were striking.

I spun from the body and rummaged in my fridge, finding another carton of juice. Fueling up before I go memory diving. Maybe it would stave off the blacking out?

"Okay, here we go," I told the corpse. I pulled my gloves off, stepped back up and wrapped my hand around her wrist. My vision tunneled and spat me out in Hayley's mind. I was running through the forest. A squeal of laughter and excitement burst from my throat as I wove between the trees and dodged the fallen woodland, the branches sticking in my feet like little spikes. I darted behind a fallen tree and collapsed behind it, my heart beating fast. *Jake wouldn't find me*, the thought flitted across my mind. That was new, I didn't normally have thoughts.

I smiled as the branches gave way to my pursuer. He circled past me to the left and I contemplated whether I should remain hidden or make a run for it. Silence blanketed the forest, making me tilt my head. Even the slight breeze was muted.

"Hayley," the air breathed my name from every direction. My breath caught in my throat. That wasn't Jake, that was something else, something other, something deadly. Darkness obscured the moon herself, and the world fell into deep shadows. I could barely see my hand in front of my face.

A pressure built around my throat, my hands clambered around it trying to pry the shadows that threatened to consume my soul. Tears swam in my eyes as Jake stepped towards me, his features melting into the devil himself, and within his eyes I knew utter and complete terror. He smiled, revealing sharp teeth and a wicked intent. A wave of recognition played at the edges of my mind, his features shimmering in and out of focus as he slinked closer to me. The pressure ramped up, pressing on the sides of my throat. He wasn't strangling me; he was starving my brain of the vital oxygen it needed. I was stroking out.

Oxygen shoved its way into my lungs, dragging a starving woman back from the edge. My eyes burst open and my hands grabbed my throat, ensuring the grasp had gone. I squinted against the bright light; the brief thought that I had been dead floated through my mind. A steady thump, thump, thump indicated a lump was forming on the back of my head. I was on the floor… again. Maybe I should install a cushioned floor?

That was a new experience. Hayley had died a horrible, terrorizing death. But the important thing was, she had died an unnatural death. Dave had some explaining to do. I grabbed the edge of the slab, careful not to touch Hayley. No way I wanted to relive that. I dragged myself up; the room swayed to the left. My eyes closed, and I waited for the nausea to subside, then shuffled my way to the office door.

Rebecca sat on the edge of the chaise longue, her ankles crossed and her hands resting on one knee. Dave paused in his pacing and spun to face me. "Two hours," he grumbled. "Two hours, whilst I had to wonder what the hell was happening."

I made it next to Rebecca and plonked myself down. The White Furry Menace shot from under my desk and into my lap. Her claws digging into my thighs as she made me her personal cushion.

"Nice to see you too," I mumbled, leaning back. She turned, giving me her back, wrapped her tail around her body, and settled on my lap like a loaf of bread.

Dave grabbed one of the visitor's chairs and dragged it in front of me. He glanced at Rebecca; she rolled her eyes, stood and left the room. "How did she die?" Dave asked.

"Pressure on her carotid artery, she stroked out."

He tilted his head. "What else?"

"Was she found in the woods?"

He nodded. "Yes."

"She was out there with someone named Jake, not the guy you had in here earlier."

Dave's eyes hardened as he went through a mental list of the shifters in the pack. "I don't know a Jake."

"Well, that's what she called him, but he changed, morphed into the same entity that Daniel saw before he died."

Dave nodded. "I'll look into the name."

"How long has this been going on?"

He ran a hand down his face, when he lifted his eyes to meet mine he'd aged twenty years. "Six months minimum, maybe twelve."

I reeled back. "And you waited until now to tell me?"

His jaw ticked. "I didn't know you were a retro or I would have engaged your services sooner."

He had me there. "It's not something I advertise."

"So this Jake was hunting her?"

I shook my head. "She was out there willingly. They were playing a game. She was excited until he changed."

Dave stared into my eyes, his dangerous gaze trying to dig for more secrets. "You could sense how she was feeling? Is that normal?"

"Normal is relative. My retro ability is specifically attuned to the moments before death. Up to now, I have not experienced unnatural death."

"Call it what it is, murder."

"I need to know more about the other deaths. Do you think they are linked?"

His face shut down and blanked. "No, you just need to do the job I'm paying you for."

At this point he should be glad the White Furry Menace had taken up residence on my lap, otherwise I may have introduced him to the furious fists of Cora Roberts.

"Every time I touch one of these people, I take my life into my own hands. Do you know how dangerous it is?"

He raised his eyebrows and leaned forward. "No, tell me."

"If I experience one of these unnatural deaths and my brain convinces itself it's me that is dying—that's it, I'm gone."

He blinked and tilted his head. "This can kill you?"

I gave a sharp nod. "The more information I arm myself with, the less likely I am to fall into the trap of thinking it's real."

He sucked his bottom lip between his teeth. "I can't give you the information you are looking for, it's above my paygrade to make that kind of decision."

"Then find me someone who can, because until then I'm not looking at another body for you."

CHAPTER NINE

A shifter, a vampire, and a sheriff walk into a bed and breakfast...

Seven blissful hours of sleep and four helpings of leftover lasagna later, I was ready to face whatever else Thursday was going to throw at me. Little did I know that thought would bite me in the ass less than ten minutes later. My phone vibrated on the table.

Dangerous Dave: Heads up. I will be bringing a representative to answer your questions shortly.

The boundary wards clanged in my head. Ha-ha, Dave, thanks for the twenty-second warning.

"Cora," Rebecca's voice floated from down the hallway. I gulped the last of my juice, checked my white T-shirt for slops. Nope, all good here.

I shoved away from the table and made my way to greet Dave and his higher up pal. Rebecca danced around the front door, her pretty pale blue sundress floating around her. I glanced at the empty front desk as I walked past it. Huh, Maggie was missing.

I came to a stop next to Rebecca. Maybe this wasn't Dave and his pal. "Why are you looking so wound up? Please tell me this isn't another scorned woman wielding a shotgun. I just repaired the last bullet hole."

Rebecca frowned, then shook her head. I flung the door open, ready to greet the representative of the pack. My brain faltered as I spied the powerful male striding towards me in a similar outfit to the last time we met. Henley shirt and jeans. Our eyes met and recognition smacked me in the face like a wet fish. My mouth fell open. He tilted his head, a small smirk playing on his lips. Rebecca peeked over my shoulder, her breath hitching. "Why is the Terror of Tennessee here?"

My head snapped to her. "What?" No, this could not be the pack Principal also known by apt names such as The Terror of Tennessee and the Louisiana Leviathan after destroying entire packs of rogue shifters single handedly. Rogues weren't the same as loners. Neither belonged to a pack, but rogues attacked humans and didn't care if their identity became known to the world. They threatened the fabric of the supernatural society and needed to be dealt with swiftly. The arrogant male who had sat across from me in a creaky plastic chair could not be the leader of the North American packs.

"I think this is the pack representative," I mumbled, stepping out onto the porch.

"Representative? He's freaking God to them."

His stride ate up the six steps to the door like he owned the house, not me. The hairs on my arms stood on end in warning. Good lord, he was tall. I mean, everyone over the age of thirteen was tall to me. But he was a freaking mountain. I thrust out my hand; he looked down at it, then at me. "I'm looking for The Undertaker." He glanced over my head, no doubt seeking my alter ego that would satisfy his conception.

Stupid nickname. I continued to offer my hand and gritted out, "Cora Roberts."

"Hudson Abbot, and I'm still looking for The Undertaker." Perhaps I should get one of those little magnetic name badges. He glanced at my hand and his smile turned hard as he waited for The Undertaker to appear and bow to his lordship. Oh, the irony. He shook my hand once and dropped it.

"Is he in?" he asked.

Dave jogged up the path. His gaze flicked between me and the Principal. "You've met Cora," he stated.

Hudson frowned. I rolled my eyes, whilst Dangerous Dave clamped his lips together and ran a hand over them, hiding his smirk. Thanks Dave, not only was I fighting a nickname, but a sexist view of expectation. Reality was about to bitch slap his holiness.

Dave gestured to me. "Hudson Abbot, meet Cora Roberts, The Undertaker." I glanced at him. He couldn't resist needling me.

"She's a girl," Hudson pointed out. The Principal shifter, ladies and gentleman.

"What did you expect? A burly man with tattoos and WWE title belts gracing the wall?"

"That would have been closer to expectations, yes."

I stepped aside, not wanting this conversation in the blistering heat of the Louisiana afternoon. "Well then, consider me breaking the mold. Would you like to come in?"

His steps bore a coiled focus, ready for threats as he assessed his surroundings. His face gave away nothing. I turned my back on him and waltzed into my home, down the stairs and into my office, the faint mumbling of two shifter males behind me.

I dropped into my chair and waved my hand at the chairs opposite. The two males folded themselves into the seats, Rebecca closing the door behind them.

I eyed Dave and gave him the hard-assed Roberts' stare he hadn't experienced before. He had the decency to look a little sheepish. Then I turned my glare on Hudson.

"If you wish me to continue to help look into pack deaths, then I need more details," I said.

Hudson narrowed his eyes. "Why?"

I glanced at Dave. He shrugged like he hadn't told him anything, other than my refusal to help any further. He made me look like a toddler stamping my feet to get more attention. I settled my hands on the desk in front of me and met the Principal's gaze head on.

"I'm a retro." Hudson stilled as I continued. "With a gift finely attuned to someone's death. Every time I use my gift, I risk getting lost in the pain and terror. I have to actively convince my brain it is not us dying."

"And how would having more information help you counter that?"

"Because the less off guard I am, the less likely I am to get dragged under." He narrowed his eyes. I held off rolling mine. "When you first watch a scary movie and you don't know what's going to happen—it makes you jump more and seem scary, right?"

He shrugged. "Sure."

"But the next time you watch it, you know what's going to happen—so it's less terrifying. If I know what to expect, at least to a certain degree, then I will be less involved in the actual memory. So far this week I've had a heart attack and a stroke."

Hudson folded his arms, his Henley shirt pulling across his biceps. "We've had at least twelve pack deaths we

113

suspect are linked to whatever is happening. The first deviation was the loner, Daniel." Twelve, wow, that was insane. And unless they wanted to exhume the bodies, all would be inaccessible to me.

"Any links other than them being pack members and unexplained?" I asked.

Hudson shook his head. "No."

I turned to Dave. "Any luck on discovering who Jake is?"

He shook his head. "There's no Jake in the pack. He must have been a loner."

"If he was ever a shifter to begin with," I mumbled.

Hudson unraveled his arms, placed his elbows on his knees and leaned forward. "You don't think he was a shifter?"

I shrugged. "Did you scent any unfamiliar shifters on Hayley?"

Hudson glanced at Dave. "No," Dave answered.

"So he was someone who could make himself appear as a shifter?" Hudson asked.

"Which means…"

"An elemental," Hudson finished for me.

Oh boy. "Perhaps," I conceded. The boundary wards clanged in my head. More visitors. I glanced at my watch. Perhaps it was the paper delivery boy? Thursday was The Chronicle delivery day.

"Don't cover up for your own kind."

I blinked. "I'm not; I've said I will help. I want these killings to stop as much as you. Needless death disturbs me on a level you can't even begin to understand."

"It wouldn't be the first time an elemental had gone on a serial killer spree."

"All supernatural species have their villains, yours included."

"Name one."

Pain flared across my abdomen and it took everything I had not to rub that spot. I rolled my shoulders to fight off the need to take my true form. "You have a bloody, brutal history yourself."

"You're calling me a serial killer?"

"You have killed many people in the name of your own justice."

"They broke the rules," Hudson scoffed.

"How many pack members have received this kind of justice when they stepped out of line?"

"Stepping out of line and threatening our existence are two very separate things."

"That's a matter of perception and also how far over the line the pack member stepped."

"We don't tolerate killers in or out of the pack."

I slammed my hand on the desk as heat flushed through my body. My muscles quivered in anticipation of a fight. "You are so busy looking at black and white, you are missing all the shades of gray. There are worse things than death."

He narrowed his eyes. I glanced at Dave, who was also giving me a curious stare. Reel it back, Cora. You are making it personal and exposing your weakness to the predators before you. "Who are you referring to?" Hudson drawled, leaning back and studying me. His relaxed stance meant to lure me into sharing.

I laughed. Excellent, now I looked like a madwoman. "I just think that your pack laws could do with updating."

"Well pack politics aside, I have little more I can tell you about the deaths. No obvious cause of death. Externally they looked like they just dropped dead."

I sucked in a breath. "Fine."

"Fine?" Dave said.

"I'll continue to help."

Rebecca burst through the door. The Terror of Tennessee twisted in his chair. Dangerous Dave kept his focus on me. Somehow I warranted the bigger threat despite the Vampire Princess in the room. She cleared her throat. "Sebastian is here, he has something urgent to discuss with you."

I frowned. "I'll be there shortly. Please see him to the parlor."

She nodded and trotted back upstairs; the door clicking shut behind her. "Unless there is anything else you can tell me, we are done."

"If we get another body, you should come to them," Hudson said.

I stood, putting me a few inches above him. "I'm not a crime scene investigator."

"No, but you might see something we are missing."

I sighed. "I won't be performing a retro read anywhere but my lab."

"Why?" Hudson drawled.

"Because she's vulnerable," Dave answered. I glared at him. "I suspect she has zero awareness of her surroundings during the reads, and afterwards she passes out cold."

I resisted the urge to slow clap. "I'll think about visiting your scenes."

I stepped around the desk and made my way to the door, swinging it open and arching an eyebrow at the pair.

They stood in unison, Dave stalking past me first. I wouldn't meet his eyes. He wasn't my friend; he was an acquaintance with an unwavering loyalty to the pack. Specifically Hudson. Hudson paused in the doorway.

"If I find out you have been keeping information from me to protect one of your own, I'll ensure you are dead to this town. No one will stay at your B&B, people won't come to you for medical help and you will no longer be in the good graces of the pack."

I stared him dead in the eyes, his alpha gaze trying to force me into submission. My knees weakened, but I would never heel. I was hardened to things much worse than an alpha stare. If he was expecting me to fall at his feet, or even with my legs open, he was shit out of luck. "I understand." His eyes tightened.

I followed them up the stairs. Now for the tricky part, getting rid of shifter royalty and replacing it with whatever vampire issues had arrived at my door. Sebastian wasn't prone to dramatics, and he rarely called upon me unannounced.

I got them past the still empty reception desk, and to the door. I held my breath as Dave reached for the front door handle. He turned and looked at Hudson.

"Weren't you saying just this week you needed to strengthen your relations with the vampires?"

Hudson's head bobbed. No way, they weren't hijacking my friendship with Sebastian. I also wasn't a halfway house for supernatural political meetings.

"Do it on your own time," I said.

"It's fine, Cora," Sebastian said as he entered the room with a casual swagger. Hudson and Dave spun around, their postures tense as they faced off with their genetic enemy. I swung my gaze to Sebastian as he reached up to adjust his navy tie. To a casual observer, it was a move to ensure one's appearance was impeccable. To me it was Sebastian screaming, *fuck my life, I have to put on a show for the shifters.*

"Either you're here to drag me into vampire shenanigans or someone's dead," I said.

He gave me a puzzled look. "How do you know?"

"You're wearing your lucky tie - the one you wear when you need something from someone and you're not sure how to go about getting it."

"My vote's on shenanigans," Rebecca announced, appearing next to him. On paper, these two looked like the perfect couple. Their lineage provided a genetic compatibility that meant they would produce the perfect heirs. More importantly, it would unite two powerful countries.

"Are you blind? How many dead bodies have been turning up around here lately?" Maggie's voice echoed around the room. Ah, she was at the desk, she was just hiding beneath it... from Hudson.

"It's both, actually. I need you to help me bury a body," Sebastian said. Why me? Did I have *Cora Roberts, supernatural grave digger* on my resume? If I didn't, I should.

I shook my head, massaged my temples, and swept past him into the parlor. I threw myself into the armchair and

120

waited for the group of shifters and vampires to take their seats.

"What happened?" I asked Sebastian.

"Do you remember Great Aunt Louisa?"

I nodded. "Your crazy aunt who lives on the outskirts of town. She runs the 'Helping Vampires to Blend into Society' group in the local church?"

Hudson smothered a laugh. "There are so many things wrong with that statement."

I ignored him. Sebastian did the same as he continued. "This afternoon was meant to be the celebration of this year's group successfully inserting themselves into the human world."

A shiver of dread worked its way up my spine. "Okay."

"But when Aunt Louisa arrived to set up, one of the group, Harry Forte, was dead."

"Dead?" Rebecca asked. My thoughts froze.

"How old?" I asked. Vampires, like all living creatures, had an expiration date. It was just lengthy.

"Forty two."

Practically a teenager. "How?"

Sebastian ran a hand through his hair. "I don't know, it looks like he just dropped dead." I caught Hudson's eyes. He was doing the math, just like me. "Harry is in your lab."

My head snapped back to Sebastian. Only he would dare go into my lab without my permission, but it still irked me. "Why?" He glanced between the shifters. I waved my hand. "You can be candid, they know about my gift."

He nodded. "House Elliot would like to employ your services in the matter of Harry Forte's death."

My head collapsed back on the chair, and my eyes closed. My energy was drained with my own responsibilities and playing pack mortician. Now the vampires wanted to weigh in. I'm not sure I would survive the week. Retro reads were usually a month or two apart. But if the vampires discovered I was providing aid to the shifters but refusing them, they would blacklist my residence for all vampires. House affiliated or not. "How soon?" I asked.

"House Elliot would like to know if there was foul play involved immediately so we can track the culprit and bring them to justice."

I peeled one eye open and gave him my best death stare. "You know it involved foul play otherwise you wouldn't be here."

Sebastian flicked his gaze at Dave. "I want to know if it is linked to any other suspicious deaths in the area." Translation—has whatever is hunting shifters now turned their attention to vampires? "Harry was the head of House Forte, after you have conducted your examination, I will take him home for burial."

Hudson leaned forward. "You think whatever killed our shifters killed your vampire?"

Sebastian blinked. "It would be unwise to not consider the possibility."

Hudson's gaze swung to me. "So the only faction not targeted would be the elementals."

I rolled my eyes. "Yes, of course, the evil elementals did it."

"So you admit it's a possibility?"

"At this point, all we have is a shadowy form that can mimic a shifter and kill without leaving a mark on the body. We have no motive, no weapon, we don't even have a thread that connects the victims."

"Except they aren't elementals," Hudson said.

The clang of the wards in my mind signals yet another visitor. What now? All beings with supernatural hearing twist their heads to the front door.

"Expecting visitors?" Dave said, standing.

I peeled myself from the armchair. "I run a bed and breakfast and a medical clinic for supernaturals. I always expect visitors."

Three raps of someone's knuckles against the front door sounded through the room. "Human," Rebecca mumbled.

"Male," Dave added.

"Thanks for the heads up," I muttered while strolling past them.

I flung the door open and came face to face with Sheriff Robert Peterson. The night was beginning to bruise the sky and chase the sun to its slumber. "Sheriff," I greeted.

"Miss Roberts, may I come in?"

I stepped back and waved him into the lobby. I closed the door and sorted out my thoughts. I had the Vampire Prince of North America, The Principal of the North American packs, and now the local sheriff in my home. This was adding up to be a swell day.

"How can I help you?" I asked. His dark eyes took in everything he could see from his position in the reception area. The sheriff had strong features and copper skin that spoke of mixed heritage. He kept his head shaved in a military cut. It looked good on him.

Maggie chose that moment to poke her head up from behind the desk. "Do you need to book a room, Sheriff?" I sent her a death glare. No, Maggie, we didn't offer humans a room at the supernatural inn. I wouldn't be able to explain everything that happened in this house in the light of day, never mind the dead of night.

He frowned at Maggie. "No, thank you." He was out of uniform, dressed in jeans and a short-sleeved blue linen shirt, probably on his way home. This wasn't an official call. He swung his gaze to me. "I've had a few reports of unusual vehicles entering your premises."

I tilted my head just as Rebecca floated into the room, a coy smile on her lips. Thanks Rebecca, but I don't think Sheriff Peterson is going to be blinded by your womanly ways. Proving me right. He didn't even acknowledge her presence as she carried on down the stairs. Clever girl. "What vehicles?"

"Large vans, in the middle of the night."

Thanks Dave. "Deliveries," I said.

"Of what?"

"Is this an interrogation? Am I a suspect?"

"For what?" he asked. Oh, well played.

"Are large vans only allowed to drive around between the hours of 7 am and 7 pm?"

He held my gaze, not even a blink. "When was the last time you received a delivery?"

"Last night."

"So what did the large black sack contain that was brought into the lower floor of the house thirty minutes ago?"

"Flour."

He blinked. I waved at Maggie who was sitting openly gawking at the pair of us. "Maggie likes to bake."

He glanced at her smiling face. Then stepped to the left, I twisted to follow him. What are you up to? He gazed over my shoulder, straight into my parlor. "Guests?"

I glanced over my shoulder. Hudson stood with a grace seen only in feline shifters, Dave followed, with Sebastian two steps behind him. They congregated in the reception

126

area, shrinking the large space with their alpha bullshit posturing. Sheriff Peterson looked unimpressed. I could sympathize. I needed to get rid of the curiosity-ridden Sheriff and throw him off the scent of any weird happenings at Summer Grove House. The problem with Robert was he was like a dog with a bone, and he'd been that way since he was a child. He grew up in one of the epicenters of the supernatural world with zero knowledge of it. His senses told him something was off, his skills threw facts at him he couldn't explain in his narrow human view of the world. Most people explained away the unexplainable; Robert had no such faults and therefore presented a threat. He'd been the Sheriff for ten months, 6 months longer than his predecessor who split the moment two and two didn't add to make four. Robert, however, liked mysteries, and White Castle was uniquely full of them. The previous long-term sheriff was human but native to White Castle and had slowly sunk into the supernatural world and policed us all the better for it. Robert was still working out why the bears around here seemed overly friendly and the wolves overly large. But I had high hopes that even when he knew what went bump in the night, he would stick around and judge people as friend or foe based on their personalities, not species. Because if he didn't then the two leaders he was currently facing would remove him if he continued to assert himself as a threat. He had two choices for survival; leave his suspicions the hell alone, or be welcomed into the inner circle and become one of the few humans who knew of our existence. It wasn't uncommon in local law enforcement, but it required the agreement of appointed representatives of all three factions. Luckily for the Sheriff, all three representatives stood before him now. If he kept this up, we would have a choice to make.

I smiled my best innocent smile. "Is there anything else I can help you with, Sheriff?" I asked.

He studied each of the alpha males, no doubt committing their faces to memory for future reference and identification. Maggie gave Hudson a nervous smile as she ambled past us, a stack of colorful flyers in her hands. The Sheriff glanced down and peeled one from her hands. "You're holding a singles night?" he asked, his eyebrows creeping up.

Maggie smiled up at him. "Yes, you should come."

The Sheriff smiled back, calculating. Excellent, then he would have access to the house to snoop around and pay attention to the supernaturals trying to find matches for the evening, whether to scratch their itch or find a longer term commitment. "I'll do just that," he drawled.

"Then I guess we will be seeing you next Sunday evening," I said.

He folded the flyer and shoved it in his back pocket. "You can count on it." He spun on his heel and opened the front door. "Good evening, gentlemen, Cora."

The door clicked shut, and I spun on a retreating Maggie. "Maggie…"

She spun towards me, her silky hair swishing. She blinked her big brown eyes. "Yes?" How can she not understand the problem?

"You just invited the Sheriff to our singles evening?"

She nodded. "Yes, he was giving you the eyes." Her eyes went comically wide.

I frowned. "He was not giving me any eyes but suspicious ones, and you just invited him to spend an evening with horny single vampires and shifters."

Rebecca reappeared from the stairs. "He was definitely giving you the eyes."

I folded my arms. "Just because his eyes weren't glued to your ass, doesn't mean he was interested in me."

Sebastian chuckled. "He was giving you the eyes."

Hudson tilted his head. I glared at him and dared him to say something about the singles evening given where we'd met. I wondered if Dave knew. Come to think of it, why the hell was the Principal in a human dive bar chatting up human women? Dave smothered a laugh. My gaze snapped to him. "There were no eyes!"

"Anyway, you can dazzle him with your personality next Sunday, maybe test out his views on things that go bump in the night," Sebastian said.

I needed them to refocus on the dead bodies and not my love life, or nonexistent love life. "Speaking of things that go bump in the night, I should go visit Harry and see what he has to say for himself."

"The Sheriff hasn't left," Hudson muttered, stroking his 5 o'clock shadow. He pulled men's grooming off with an effortless flair. "You should consider having that conversation in a different location."

Great, I had a snooping Sheriff and a dead vampire on the premises. At least Dave had taken Hayley's body back to the pack. The wards surrounding my makeshift graveyard persuaded prying eyes to look elsewhere. I was confident that part of my property was safe. Rebecca tapped my arm. "I think you should take the Bugatti when you go to visit Harry."

Sebastian's eyes widened. She'd stored the dead vampire in the trunk of his custom Bugatti.

"I think we should join you," Dave said.

I shook my head. "That's okay, I will report the details of the conversation to you." Wow, speaking in code was hard.

"I'll be joining you. Dave, go back and ensure security is as tight as can be," Hudson asserted.

I threw my hands up. "Fine, group outing to – " I raised an eyebrow at Sebastian.

"I have a place." Of course he did. The Vampire Prince of North America knew where to store dead bodies.

Chapter Ten

The worst pickup lines are spoken whilst flat on your back

with a strong man between your thighs.

I'd gotten two steps down to the basement when I realized I had not one, but two males on my tail. I paused and glanced over my shoulder, fixing Hudson with a hard stare. "Where do you think you're going?"

"We just agreed I would accompany you both to examine the body."

"How do you think you are getting there?"

"In your car?"

I glanced at Sebastian, whose lips twitched. "I drive a two-seater custom Bugatti. There are three of us, and the trunk is occupied."

Hudson took a few steps down, past Sebastian before landing next to me. "Then I guess you'll have to make yourself comfortable on my knee, sweetheart, because there's no way I'm letting you out of my sight until we have answers."

"It's my car."

"Actually..." Sebastian cut in. I glared at him. "What she said, it's her car."

"So?" Hudson said, folding his arms.

"So, I drive. It's not me you'll be making comfortable on your knee," I nodded at Sebastian. "It's him."

I trotted down the stairs, through my office and lab. I snagged the keys from the hook before pushing open the garage door. The males followed me and some hushed argument took place. I clicked the doors unlocked and opened the driver's side door. I leant on the door frame whilst the crème de la crème of the supernatural male species figured out who was riding shotgun.

133

Sebastian straightened his already straight tie, a set of silver keys dangling from his left hand. "I'll be driving Hudson's vehicle, you can follow." Translation, Hudson didn't trust me not to leave him eating Bugatti dust, so he was hitching a ride with me.

I dropped into the leather seat and parked my oversized sunglasses on my nose. The Terror of Tennessee folded himself next to me with far less finesse. Serves his over-muscled majesty right - he should stick to driving his own car. A sleek black Range Rover stormed the gravel in front of us, throwing up stones sharp enough to chip paintwork. I hoped he was insured.

Sebastian took a right out of Summer Grove House, away from White Castle and sped towards the I-10 which connected a small smattering of towns from White Castle to New Orleans.

"You really don't know where the vampire is going?" Hudson broke the silence by calling me a liar. Smooth.

"Nope," I popped the P, dropped the gear and sped up to catch a retreating Sebastian.

"So a Vampire Prince and a backward town elemental B&B owner?"

"Huh?" Where was he going with this?

"Are you together?"

I smothered a laugh. "No. We are not."

"Then why is he at your house asking favors and moving around you with a familiarity reserved for family?"

"Sebastian is as good as family, we are friends." And I could count those on one hand.

"Huh." I glanced over just as Hudson twisted his body towards me and stared.

"What?"

"Vampires don't normally fraternize with elementals."

"We do."

"How did you meet?"

"Medical school."

"You're an actual doctor?"

I nodded. "You think I treat people with the supernatural version of WebMD?"

"Is there a supernatural version?"

"No."

"So you run a B&B, check out shifter loner deaths for me-"

"Dave," I corrected. "I do it for Dave, not you."

135

He waved a hand in my periphery. "Same difference, and you run a medical clinic for supernaturals?"

"That sums me up, yes." That's right, nothing to see here, just a boring elemental with a weird gift.

"Somehow I doubt that."

I sighed and followed Sebastian off a side road that quickly morphed into a dirt track. Now the car would need cleaning. Great. "I don't want to encourage you, but that's all there is to know."

I pointed at the glove compartment. "Could you pass me the glucose tablets please?" He popped the compartment and paused before rummaging through the twenty packs.

"Orange cream, wild berry or cherry?"

"Wild berry."

He grabbed a pack and peeled it open. I held my right hand out. He dropped two tablets in my palm.

"Why were you at The Pit?" he asked.

A smirk appeared on my face as I threw the tablets in my mouth and tapped on the steering wheel with my hand. "Sebastian bet me this beauty for another month that I couldn't last the full fifteen males. He lost."

I glanced at him. "Why were you at The Pit?"

"Looking for a date."

I highly doubted that, but his secrets were his to own. I wasn't interested. "Another four please," I said as a rundown two-story concrete monstrosity appeared in front of us. A worn and battered sign declared it as once being the site of White Castle Hospital. Except the W and H had long since disappeared.

"He's a classy bastard." He dropped the tablets in my outstretched hand.

"He's resourceful," I countered. "Nobody for miles, the building was abandoned over ten years ago. No security patrols the barren concrete box."

"A perfect place to examine a dead vampire."

My lips twitched. "Is the kitty afraid of the dead?"

"No one likes the dead, Cora."

I wove between the debris littered around the parking lot and pulled to a stop behind the Range Rover.

I unclipped my seat belt and popped another four glucose tablets in my mouth. "The dead can't hurt us. It's the living who perform acts of unspeakable evil." I climbed out of the car, pushing my sunglasses onto the top of my head, and met an exasperated Sebastian. He threw Hudson the keys

137

and rounded the Bugatti, popping the trunk. Harry Forte was wrapped in a thick black body bag. You couldn't fault the vampires for being thorough. No cheap black sacks or sheets for their dead. Sebastian threw the bag over his shoulder and strode towards the smashed glass doors that led us into the hospital.

Hudson fell into step beside me, a frown marring his face. He wasn't attractive in the same way as Sebastian. His nose was slightly out of shape, and a scar ran through his left eyebrow, leaving a bald line. His bottom lip was fuller than his top. He wore his hair on the longer side, styled on top of his head, highlights from being out in the Louisiana sunshine shimmering throughout the dark brown strands. Sebastian was pretty, Hudson was rugged, capable. Ugh, I bet he had calloused hands. Okay, brain, back in the game—dead vampires, not shifter kings with an ego the size of the state. We entered the reception area, once a clean and clinical building with perpendicular lines. Now nature had reclaimed its world. Trees poked through the damaged roof, vines of various plants spilled through the windows and onto the floor. A woodsy scent had long since eradicated the stringent scent of antiseptic.

Sebastian caught hold of a stray stretcher in the lobby and laid the body bag onto it. He pushed it deeper into the hospital, the left front wheel protesting with a squeak that set my teeth on edge. He led us away from the sunlight, down a darkened hallway, and swung a left. I went to grab my phone from my pocket.

"Shit," I grumbled.

"What's wrong?" Hudson asked.

"I forgot my phone, and unlike you and Sebastian, I don't have night vision." On cue, I tripped over some unseen object. Hudson's arm shot out and banded around my waist. He steadied me against his hard chest. This wouldn't do. I debated climbing on the trolley with the dead vampire. That's how much I wanted to avoid being body to body with him. He peeled his arm from around me and grabbed my hand. Huh, guess that would work too. Except, goddammit, he had calloused hands.

We picked our way through rubble, Sebastian forcing the trolley with his vampire strength until we approached the end of the corridor that ended in a set of double doors. A sign announced it as theatre 1. This would work. I could perform a retro read anywhere, but he was trying to recreate my lab conditions to give me a sense of familiarity. He rounded the trolley, pushed the door open with his butt and backed into the room. We followed and my first problem became clear.

"There's no light in here," I pointed out.

"Do you need light?" Hudson asked.

"Well no, but it's normal to want to see what the hell I'm doing. Plus, I don't just perform a retro read, I check the body carefully for signs of what happened."

"To prepare you?"

"Yes."

"So you are less likely to succumb to the death memory?"

"A plus, congrats, you have an excellent memory."

A stream of yellow light burst from the right corner of the room, temporarily blinding me. It angled itself away from me and on to the metal slab where the black bag now lay. "Sorry," Sebastian said, laying the flashlight on the cabinet. He grabbed another one from a drawer and positioned it on the other side of the room. The third one, he handed to me.

"You want me to stay?" he asked as I stood next to the body bag.

I shook my head. "No, both of you need to wait outside. I've filled up on glucose tablets so I'm hoping the passing out part won't come until later."

Sebastian handed me a pair of gloves he must have snagged on his way through my lab. "Thank you," I said, snapping them on.

"Don't you need skin to skin contact to do the read?" Hudson asked as I unzipped the bag, the yellow flashlight highlighting the waxy complexion of Harry Forte.

"What I need is for you to leave me alone."

Hudson folds his arms, a protest forming on his lips. Sebastian shook his head. "She won't even let me stay, and we have been through thick and thin together."

Hudson's eyes tightened, I stepped back from the operating table. I wouldn't be bullied, I was from a strong elemental line of women whose mantra centered on never being forced to do anything, especially by a man. "The quicker you leave, the faster you will get answers."

His jaw ticked. A sixty-second standoff occurred with his hazel eyes flashing alpha at me. I cocked an eyebrow despite the pressure on me to submit. He dropped his arms with a sigh. "Fine, I will be right outside these doors."

"No, you can go sit in reception with Sebastian."

He stormed through the door muttering about awkward women with a god complex. Sebastian's lips twisted into a smile. "What are you smirking at?" I asked as he backed away to the door.

He shrugged. "There were definitely eyes."

I rolled my eyes. "There were no eyes from the sheriff, and even if there were, it would be a terrible idea to start something with a man who I had to hide half of my life from." As it was, I had to hide a significant part of myself from everyone. Dating outside of the supernatural arena would be twice the work.

He grinned. "I wasn't talking about the sheriff." He spun with a wink and waltzed out of the room. I blinked and stared at Harry.

"If he wasn't talking about the sheriff, who was he talking about?" I muttered to the dead vampire. He didn't answer back. Hmm... I wondered where his ghost was. Back at the house I had a soul stone in my rooms, which would compel nearby wandering spirits to hang out there until I made it to them. But we weren't at the house, which meant Harry's spirit was wandering around this hospital somewhere.

I peeled the black bag away and revealed a slim man dressed in smart grey slacks, a white button down and a corduroy jacket. His blonde hair was receding and his eyebrows needed a trim. He wore a plain gold band on his wedding finger. A faint whiff of vanilla floated from him, a typically female scent.

I examined him from head to toe, not finding anything to suggest what had caused this seemingly healthy vampire to drop dead in a church. I dragged a deep breath in and rolled my gloves off.

"I hope you didn't die painfully," I muttered at Harry and grabbed his arm.

My vision sank into darkness and I blinked my eyes open. The sun shone through the stained glass window, creating a kaleidoscope of colors on the mottled marble floor. I walked towards a small table laden with a boiler, cups, and various pastry treats. I placed the cookies I'd brought with me on the table and reminded myself that I must take the plate back home at the end, otherwise Martha would have my balls. A smile pulled at my lips as I thought of my wife back home. She was proud of my achievements in this group. I had a mechanic's job at the local garage; my boss liked me

143

and I hadn't fed from him. That was my biggest achievement.

The door creaked open. It could use some WD-40. I glanced at my watch; it was my turn to set up. I spun and watched as a cloaked figure made their way up the aisle. Ric was here early. He was a sponsor for a new member of the group. Ric didn't feel right, he made me nervous, but I'd let it slide, not wanting to stick my nose into anyone else's business. He glided towards me, the hood of his cloak shielding his face.

"Good morning, Ric, you're early. The others won't be here for at least another forty-five minutes."

Ric's head tilted up and his hood slid down. Recognition slapped me in the face, and I sucked in a breath. But this wasn't Harry's thoughts—these were mine, I knew him. Ric wasn't a vampire, he was an elemental. A high-ranking officer of the Order. My mind tried to connect the dots as the death memory continued to play out. Why was he here? Was he investigating the murders? That's all we needed, the Order sticking their busybody noses in where they don't belong.

Ric's stormy blue eyes narrowed on me. "Cora," he said, rolling the r with a growl.

"Who?" Harry said.

My mind zeroed in on Ric. "It took me numerous bodies to uncover the Princess of Death. But now I have your attention, we need to discuss what you need to do for me." Princess of Death? That's a new one. I'll stick with The Undertaker.

"I will do nothing for a murderer," I ground out. How was this happening? How was I speaking? Were we actually communicating right now, or was he premeditating what I would think?

He sighed and tilted his head, the gelled brown spikes staying still. "You are wondering how this is possible? You are out of your league, Princess, submit to my wishes and no one else needs to get hurt."

Harry's vision swept behind him, looking for the invisible princess, no doubt. He wasn't the brightest vampire in the church. "Who are you talking to?" Harry asked.

Ric's arms shot out, and he grinned like a madman, the cloak billowing around him. Ric was all about the drama, and I sensed Harry's confusion. I pulled at the collar of my shirt, a sudden heat flaring through my veins. Not the pleasant kind found at the hands of a lover. More like the 'you've been out in the sun for too long and you can hear the blood swishing through your body, too close to the skin'.

"A little canapé before I serve your main dish. Cora, do you like your food piping hot?" Ric hissed.

Sweat broke out on my forehead, palms, the nape of my neck. I fanned my face and grabbed onto the table. Black spots dotted my vision and my breath came in short pants.

"Ric, I think I'm going to pass out," Harry said breathlessly.

Ric smirked. "Where's the fun in that? I need the Princess to feel every degree as I boil your blood. I want her to feel every tear as your organs break down, and when I'm done, I want her to feel the pain that would only be the tip of the iceberg I would cause her family unless she submits to me."

I slumped, faceplanting the floor. Something hard dug into my ribs and shoved me over. I rolled to my back. I could feel my organs blistering, and tremors racked my limbs. A hoarse scream tore from my throat, the sound multi-layered as it came from both me and Harry. *It's not real, it's not real, it's not real,* I chanted. I had never felt so close to losing myself to someone else's death. My mind was struggling with reality as Ric screwed with my perception by talking to me directly.

He knelt down on one knee next to me, his face morphing into fake concern. "I can keep this up for hours, Cora, and it looks painful." Hot blood bubbled up my throat and dribbled out of my mouth. He frowned and pulled a tissue from his pocket. "Can't be having that, we need a death mysterious enough to catch your attention."

I glared at him from Harry's eyes. Death was always sad, needless death was deplorable. He did this to get my attention?

"What do you want?" I mumbled. The sound was wet. He patted around my mouth again.

"The next time I come knocking at your door? Let me in." Something vital gave way in Harry's body as we both prayed for his death. Ric's smug face was the last thing I saw before the awful agony ripped a scream straight from my throat and shocked me back into the theatre room. I held onto the table with white knuckles as I fought the urge to vomit or pass out. There was a fifty-fifty chance right now which one was going to happen. I stared at the waxy face of Harry. He had died in excruciating pain, confused and alone.

A tick, tick, tick sounded in the room. Quieter than a clock, but louder than a watch. I glanced around slowly, my eyes coming to land on Harry's torso. A glow emanated from his chest. I frowned, what on earth? The theatre door slammed open and Hudson rushed towards me just as a force propelled me backwards, my feet lifting from the floor. Hudson's body wrapped around me and tackled me to the floor, his hands cradling around my head to protect it. The ground rumbled underneath us like a T-Rex had woken up hungry. Metal screeched, the flashlights whizzed around the room before blinking out and plunging us into complete darkness. My true form yanked at its chains in a bid to protect itself, agony tearing through me as I yanked back. Dust fell into my eyes and I screwed them shut. The terrible screeching in the room halted to give way to a terrifying silence.

Hudson's hard body covered mine, his face so close that his hair was tickling my cheeks. I twisted my head to the side, my lips grazing his forearm. Awkward.

I licked my dry lips and coughed on the dust. "What the hell just happened?"

"You tell me, first with the blood-curdling screams, where I was told firmly to leave you alone. Then the bomb that you set off in the vampire."

I blinked. "Bomb?"

"We are lying under two stories of rubble, without me you would have been crushed."

Panic flared in my gut. "Sebastian?"

"He's fine, he's digging us out of here. I can hear him, he'll be awhile."

I swallowed. "Do we have enough air?"

He wiggled slightly, every inch of his hard body rubbing against mine. "Turn your head the other way, there is a trickle of fresh air making its way through."

I sighed, and the adrenaline that had been fueling one hell of a death memory, plus an explosion fled my body. In its place, I felt various shards of pain in multiple places. My left thigh was definitely wet, and my right leg felt on fire. My heart rate, however, was picking up the pace as my mind struggled to come to terms with how trapped we were.

"Are you injured?" he asked.

"I'll survive." I wriggled my leg. I needed room and space. I needed to breathe. "Could we try side by side as opposed to you on top?"

I could practically feel his grin despite not being able to see a thing. My cheeks flushed. "I'm happy to try whatever position you like, but right now I think it's best I'm on top."

I frowned. "Why?"

"Because if I move, all that rubble will come tumbling down and crush you."

My heart tripped over itself in fear. I wrestled my panic attack back into its box. "Oh." Which meant he was holding up two floors of rubble on his back. Holy shit.

"And I haven't finished with you yet."

"I beg your pardon?"

"Dirty minded little witch. You still need to work out who this shadowy figure is, and he seems to have taken a dislike to you poking around his business, so until we resolve this consider your ass mine."

"No."

"You will have myself or Dave with you at all times."

"No."

"You sleep, we are there. You eat, we are there."

"What about when I pee? You have some weird fetish?"

"We are there."

"Pervert," I muttered.

"Precautious."

"Presumptuous."

He chuckled. "Confident." Metal screeched as it moved somewhere above us. The panic made a dent in its box. "You are remarkably calm for someone lying under a fallen building."

I was remarkable at hiding my genuine feelings. "When you've already lived your worst nightmare and survived, nothing much fazes you." If I could move, I would slap myself. Too much information, Cora. The silence stretched between us, disrupted by the occasional sound of rubble moving. He sagged against me, his head falling into the crook of my neck. "Hudson?" I cried out.

He laughed against my skin, giving me goosebumps. "Still here, witch. I just need to change my position. Spread your legs."

"Excuse me?"

"I'm not trying to come on to you. You are bleeding and it's causing my knee to slip. So if you open your legs, I can plant mine between them and they will stop slipping."

"If this is a chat up line, it's the worst one I've ever heard."

"Your choice, I can either end up crushing you with my body, or you can open your legs so I can maintain some distance."

I pulled in a breath. I was being an ungrateful bitch. But something about him rubbed me the wrong way. "Ready?" I asked.

"Go." He rose off me. The Principal of North America was doing a push up over my body with tons of rubble on his back. You couldn't write this shit.

I pushed my legs out as far as I could, meeting resistance on both sides. He settled back down, bringing him into direct contact with my core. I was a short ass, so at least I was wrapped around his stomach.

"Better?" I asked.

He cleared his throat; the rumble vibrating over my chest. "Yes."

His eyes flecked with amber as he gave me a helping of his alpha stare. Not the *bow to me* one. This was different. "You're creeping me out," I stated.

"Why?"

"You're staring at me with glowing eyes."

He blinked. The glow retreated. Plunging us back into darkness. He was like a personal flashlight. "Do I make you uncomfortable?" I couldn't see the smile he was wearing, but I could hear it.

"No, I'm uncomfortable because I'm fairly sure the skin of my leg has been blasted off and parts of Harry Forte are lodged in my abdomen."

"That's unfortunate."

"Indeed."

This was the most inappropriate time to find someone attractive. It was just a savior thing. As soon as we were out of this situation, we would be back to the zero attraction we felt before. "Did you get anything from your read on the vampire?" Yes, and the one thing I wouldn't be announcing is the killer's identity. I had to know for sure before I went pointing fingers at people in the Order, and my government wouldn't take kindly to me sharing it with the shifters and vampires before them.

"His blood was boiled."

"Boiled?"

"That's what I said."

"By the same shadowy figure?"

"I'm not sure."

"Hmm."

"What?"

"You don't strike me as the kind of woman to not be sure of something."

"He was cloaked."

"Cora?" Sebastian shouted from somewhere to my left.

"You think he'll shout my name with so much worry?" Hudson said.

I snorted a laugh. "Doubtful, you didn't let him sit on your knee."

"I'm okay," I shouted.

"Thank fuck for that. Hudson, you alive?"

Tiny points of light came into view as Sebastian removed more and more rubble to reach us.

"I'm alive," Hudson grumbled, as Sebastian's features came into view. Hudson tensed, then raised up and off me, brick and mortar falling from him. The pressure he'd had on so many of my wounds disappeared.

"I need a doctor," I mumbled right before I passed out.

CHAPTER ELEVEN

Doctors, honey and blood.

The doughy scent of freshly baked bread wafted around me, like coming home on a summer's day. I was lying on a cloud of soft, warm feathers. Was this heaven? When I opened my eyes, would I face my mother? My father? Huh, that would be an interesting reunion. Perhaps I should just play dead. "You're awake," a calm male baritone voice stated. Busted. I tried to roll on the cloud. My right leg protested by sending shooting agony through my spine, proving that I was, in fact, alive. My eyes peeled open, the grit from the rubble making them sticky and sore. A squat man sat on a wooden stool next to the bed I was lying on. He had greying hair, matching bushy eyebrows, and the palest of blue eyes with wrinkles crinkling in the corners. He smiled as he dipped a natural muslin cloth in a bowl of steaming water on the table and leaned forward. I spied the freshly baked bread and a glass pot with a handwritten label of 'Doc's Honey' next to the bowl and my stomach rumbled.

"Baked goods and honey after this. Close your eyes and keep them relaxed. That way I can get the dirt."

I stared at the stranger who was withholding carbohydrate goodies. "Where am I?"

"A pack owned house, 2 miles north of White Castle, and 3 miles from the hospital you were under." His southern scent was strong, honeyed with a hint of gruff.

"How long was I out?" I asked.

"Twelve hours, never seen a person sleep like the dead before." I'd slept the night away.

I pushed the blankets down and pulled up a black tank top that didn't belong to me to find my torso wrapped up tight in soft white bandages. They hid both old and new injuries. A few spots of blood seeped through. I pushed the blanket even further down. They'd dressed me in matching black shorts. I grimaced at my leg wrapped loosely in plastic wrap. That would scar.

"The cream on the burns is my special mix, you'll have a little scarring from the deepest burn. Maybe a few inches in diameter. I pulled no less than twelve fragments of vampire bones from your body. The one lodged in your liver was the biggest concern. But that will heal with rest."

"Thank you..."

"Norbert, chief medical shifter."

"Thank you, Norbert, for patching me up." I glanced around the 12 foot square room, white wash walls, no windows, two plain waxed wooden doors. "How did I get here?"

Norbert leaned back, I rubbed my eye. The door to the left swung open and Hudson ambled through, with Sebastian on his heels. They swallowed up the space in the room. "I carried you," Hudson growled out. His hair was damp, and his face flushed. Wonderful, I looked like I'd been dragged through a hedge backwards whilst his majesty was rocking the fresh out of the shower look.

My eyebrows shot up. "Carried me?"

Norbert tutted. "Yes, with three broken ribs and some nasty burns of his own."

Saved by the Terror of Tennessee. What next?

Norbert stood, handed the cloth to Hudson, and pointed at me. "She needs her eyes bathed before they become infected." He left the room muttering about stubborn females. Hudson dropped the cloth in the water and rinsed it. He sat on the stool, his enormous frame making it look ridiculous. His hand moved towards me. I stared at him. "I can do it myself."

"I know." He held the cloth inches from my eye. Sebastian leaned against the wall with a hard look set in his eyes that meant he was waging an internal battle with his emotions.

I sighed and closed my eyes. He bathed them with a gentleness I would have never expected. Rinse and repeat.

"All done," he said, the slosh of the cloth hitting water finalizing his words.

I blinked my eyes open. "Thank you."

"For what?"

"Saving me, carrying me here, getting me medical attention so I would survive, bathing my eyes."

"You're welcome. Of course, it could have been so much worse." He leaned forward, his elbows resting on his knees. He tilted his head towards Sebastian. "But the vampire's blood healed the internal injuries that would have seen you join the dead you so readily speak to."

Sebastian looked pale, even for a vampire. "You almost died in my arms," he whispered.

"Don't be so dramatic, it was a scratch," I muttered, and ultimately it would take a hell of a lot more to kill me. I rolled my shoulders, fighting the familiar ache in my body..

He flung his arms up. "I can't do this again!"

Hudson's eyes widened. Nice going, Seb. "Again?" Hudson asked, he was inconveniently observant.

"You ride off into danger with no regard for those you would hurt should you not make it," Sebastian snapped.

There was so much to unpack in that sentence. "First, it's not like I asked for it - this time or the last. Second, I looked into the death of the vampire because you asked me."

He shook his head. "Perhaps you should stop looking into deaths altogether. Whoever is doing this just upped the ante, it's not worth your life."

"I'm the only person who can look into the deaths like this, too many people are dying, he needs to be stopped."

"You have a savior complex," Hudson muttered. I shot him a glare.

Sebastian straightened with a sigh and stalked over to me before dropping a kiss on my head. "I have to head home, cousin Miranda is visiting. Don't go body investigating without me. I'll see you tomorrow at the party." He swept out of the room, the door swinging closed behind him and leaving me alone with Hudson.

"You don't seem upset about the blood," Hudson said.

Whilst vampires could take anyone's blood without consequence, sharing their blood led to an indestructible bond. Sebastian now and forever would be compelled to save my ass. He would get in the way of a pink ivory stake if it meant saving my life. Being the snobs of the supernatural world they rarely shared with anyone outside of their own species, even then it was almost exclusively between mates. "He's my best friend. I would rather be alive and bonded to someone I respect than dead."

161

He tilted his head. "It's not the first time, that explains his lack of hesitation." He was too perceptive, but he hadn't asked a question, so I offered him nothing. "When?"

Okay, Plan B, play dumb. "When what?"

He gave me a look reserved for idiots. "When did the vampire share his blood with you?"

"When the need arose."

"You often find yourself mortally injured?"

"No, this is the second time."

"And each time your vampire best friend was there?"

"No, the first time was a fortunate accident that he found me, and he wasn't my friend at the time, but I am eternally grateful that he shared his life force with me. This time I was busy investigating shifter and vampire deaths as instructed by you and him."

"Does this have anything to do with the panic attack you almost had?" He picked up on that?

I scoffed and smoothed the blankets with my hands. "Who wouldn't have a panic attack trapped under a building whilst bleeding out?"

He sighed and leaned back. I wasn't sharing the worst moment of my life with a practical stranger. We'd met less than a week ago. "What happened in the vision?" he asked.

I needed to tread very very carefully. This was a minefield. I suspected an elemental who had called me out by name. It was looking more and more likely I was the target, not the shifters or the vampires. I doubted they would take kindly to their kind being used to get to me.

"Let me help you," Hudson said, his voice dropping low. "You said his blood was boiled, that you didn't know if it was the same person because they were cloaked."

I nodded. Reducing my verbal interactions increased my chances of not fucking up. He tilted his head to the side. "What aren't you telling me?"

I had to give him something. My mind sorted through the different things, finally settling on the one that should cause me the least backlash, so long as I spun it correctly. "The figure addressed me by name."

Hudson's brow wrinkled. "He knew who you were?"

"Yes, I suspect that someone has leaked that you are bringing the murders to me for examination."

"How would he know you are a retro? It's not something you advertise."

I shrugged. "Rebecca, Sebastian and my aunts know. Two days ago Dave found out, and I suspect you knew shortly after that."

Green rolled over his irises. "Are you accusing me of leaking your abilities?"

I resisted the urge to roll my eyes. "No, but are you confident that no one overheard you and Dave discussing me?"

He narrowed his eyes. "I am very confident. Dave told me in the car as we drove to your house this morning. Before that you were The Undertaker who was helping us look into the pack deaths by examining their bodies."

"Huh." *Cora Roberts, master of the witty comeback.*

"So the better question is, why would this person be talking to you through the death memories?"

"He wasn't talking to me in real time. He knew I would look at the memory and had a one-sided, well-thought out conversation with future me."

He ran a hand over his stubble. "What did he say?"

I side stepped the landmine that was Ric's intentional murders to get my attention, to draw me out. "He wants me to invite him into my home next time he comes knocking." Oops, please don't pick up on those two words.

"Next time?"

Damn it. "The night after I examined Daniel, the boundary wards on my property were breached by someone. They tried with great gusto to enter the house. The wards protected us."

"You never mentioned this before."

"In between the dead bodies, Sheriff and the bomb?"

"You had ample time during our conversation this morning."

"We were busy ironing out my role and what you expect from me, plus you were caught up insulting my kind."

He drew in a long breath. I was testing his patience. "And in the car?"

"You were dissecting my relationship with Sebastian. Anyway, I couldn't be sure they were linked until now."

"Is that everything?" He treated me to his hard alpha stare. I wasn't totally immune, and in my weakened state it might have even sunk me to my knees had I been standing.

"That is everything you need to know," I gritted out.

"You know the reason we don't trust you elementals?" he dropped his voice, low and smooth like the softest of velvet. Yet every hair on my arm stood on end in warning. "Because of this shit. With the blood suckers we're clear; they are strong, fast, ageless and need blood. Us? We are strong, fast, have an animal side and live a long time. You? You're unpredictable, you might be able to raise the dead or mimic anyone, you could create a potion to make someone believe they're in love or see the future. That's the reason you're not trusted - not some ancient old feud nobody alive can remember the origins of."

"So you're condemning me because of the acts of a few?" He nods like he can't possibly understand how this could be wrong. "Do you realize that's how wars have started? Do you remember Samuel McBride?"

He frowns. That's right, I just slapped you with one of the worst serial killers in the world's history, and guess what? He was a shifter that murdered and raped over a hundred women from all species. "Of course."

"So I should hate all shifters because of the few bad eggs that exist in all species? I should take his acts and punish an entire population for them? You are conveniently ignoring the parallels in your attitude because you're a coward."

"I'm a coward?"

I folded my arms. "You like to control things, you like knowing all the variables and predicting all the possible outcomes."

"I'm the leader of every shifter in the North American packs, it's my job to predict outcomes and figure out solutions. It's my damn job to control everything."

He was cursing. Excellent I'm getting to him. "So, you need to admit you don't like me, not because I'm an elemental, but because I'm someone you can't figure out or control and it's freaking you out."

He scoffs. "You're not that interesting, Cora, and you're more predictable than you think."

Ouch. What a charmer. "Make your mind up. First you don't like me because I'm unpredictable, then I'm not interesting because I am predictable."

The door swung open and Dave walked in. His nostrils flared, no doubt sensing the tension. I gathered the blankets and pulled them up. "Doc wants to take a look at your ribs," Dave stated. Hudson blinked, his shoulders dropping.

167

"She knows more than she's letting on," Hudson said, vacating the stool.

"I know so much more than your tiny cat brain could comprehend," I snapped. "That doesn't mean you should be privy to it."

Hudson paused at the door and glanced over his shoulder. "I will warn you once more, if you are protecting one of your own I will – "

"Yes, yes, you'll ruin me in the town that my ancestors built. You'll tear down my livelihood so I'd have to move elsewhere." I fixed him with my hard stare. The one my grandmother had perfected in me. His gaze narrowed. "There are several holes in this threat of yours. One, the loners don't answer to you—I am often the only medical help they can find in a few hundred-mile radius. If I move, they will follow."

He opened his mouth. I sliced my hand through the air. "No." Dave stiffened as Hudson turned to give me his full attention and folded his arms. "Two, I am not one of your subjects, I don't answer to you and I don't owe you any answers. You want my loyalty, earn it. Three, I have a wealth of power at my fingertips that would boggle your mind. You

168

might turn furry and howl at the moon, but I can turn that moon crimson with the blood of my enemies. You can lie with a two story building collapsed on your back. At full strength, I can raise that building with a flick of my fingers. Don't make me an enemy, Hudson, you won't like the consequences."

He blinked, his eyes rolling with green once more. His cat was taking a long, hard look at me. A small smirk appeared on his lips as he seemed to decide something. He nodded. "Noted." He waltzed out the room.

I glanced at Dave, who looked torn between laughing and strangling me. "You just challenged the Principal of North America, Cora Roberts, I hope you are ready for what follows."

CHAPTER TWELVE

Go into the light, or not, take your pick.

We completed the ride back to my house in blissful silence. Dangerous Dave kept his opinions to himself after his declaration that I'd successfully challenged the Principal of North America. If the dead didn't kill me, Hudson Abbot would. We swung a left and pulled through the wrought-iron gates that wrapped around my estate. The boundary wards clanging in my mind. I felt like shouting, 'It's me, you idiot.'

"Expecting company?" Dave asked.

I pulled my gaze from the side window and let out a string of curses as I spied several familiar cars dumped in the drive. They were a day early. I needed rest and quiet, not an interrogation that would impress the man sitting next to me. "Family reunion."

He frowned. "I see."

No, he really didn't. I'd put money on Dave having a dossier on Cora Roberts somewhere in his neat freak office. He wouldn't work with me unless he felt he could trust me to a certain extent. That initial search would turn up the facts; a girl who never knew her father and lost her mother to depression. A fully qualified medical doctor who inherited Summer Grove House following her aunt's death with a scattering of female family members around the country who rarely got together. That is what I wanted people to find. The reality was always more twisted, deeper and complex. Him knowing my gift was enough; I didn't owe him my private life. He spun the car in a tight circle, stopping at the bottom of the steps.

"Thanks for the lift," I said, unclipping my seat belt.

"You're welcome. I have a few chores in town, then I will be back."

My head snapped to him. "Why?"

"Hudson explained we would keep you safe."

I rolled my eyes. More like Hudson was keeping a firm eye on me.

"Do you need help into the house?" Dave asked.

I shot him a look over my shoulder as I opened the car door. "I can manage."

He chuckled as I slammed the door closed. He peeled out of the driveway and out through the gates. If I stalled any longer... The front door swung open... I sighed. They would come investigate.

A tall slender woman wrapped in a designer pale blue skirt suit stepped through the door, her brunette hair cut into a classic long bob. Her regal features ensured she ruled the boardroom ruthlessly. She popped a plucked eyebrow at me as I hobbled up the stairs. They had given me a pair of sweatpants and a matching top. Aunt Liz's disgust at my attire was as clear as the Louisiana sky. A bundle of honeyed blonde hair pushed past Aunt Liz with a squeal. Aunt Dayna bounded down the stairs, her skirts jingling with hundreds of tiny metal discs, and wrapped her arms around my waist. I grimaced as she squeezed.

"Dayna, put the girl down, can't you see she's injured," Aunt Liz tsked.

Dayna dropped her arms and stood back, scanning me from head to foot. "Huh, I thought your chakra was off, but I assumed it was the man in your life making it wonky."

"No man," I told her, starting up the steps. My thigh burned as I stretched the newly forming skin. Between Sebastian's blood and the cream Norbert had applied, I was healing at a supernatural speed, which meant I needed to fuel the healing. The bread and honey had seen me home, but if I didn't give my body more to chew on soon, I'd pass out. Aunt Liz stepped out of the way, I gave her a grateful smile and limped through my front door. Maggie ran past me with a handful of blue and silver balloons. She gave me a wide-eyed look before dropping behind the reception desk, the balloons still floating in the air above her. I couldn't even right now.

The door clicked closed and my aunts flanked me as I followed the delicious scent of garlic, chicken, basil, onions... Aunt Liz was making her famous chicken soup, yum. I rounded the kitchen and found two of the six seats occupied by Rebecca and Aunt Stella, both sipping tea and no doubt sharing the latest supernatural gossip. If there was a prize for the most regal Goth, Aunt Stella would take that crown. She'd styled her deep plum hair on top of her head, her matching eyeshadow dramatic and smoky against her porcelain skin. Regardless of the weather, Aunt Stella dressed in a corset and skirt. She smiled over her cup at me as I slid into the seat opposite her.

"You're early," I said, clutching my side.

Aunt Liz glided around the kitchen before a bowl of steaming chicken soup and a hunk of fresh bread landed in front of me. She slid into the seat to my right, whilst Aunt Dayna dropped to my left. I dunked the bread in my soup. Maggie bounced into the room and took the last seat.

Aunt Liz put her cup down and steepled her fingers. "We came as soon as we got a garbled story from Maggie about a vampire prince, the Principal of North America and the local sheriff being in your residence."

"Don't forget Dangerous Dave," Maggie grinned.

I rolled my eyes. "How could I? Good news though, Maggie invited the curious human sheriff to the singles evening at the house."

The Aunt's pinned Maggie with their gaze. She clapped, clueless as they came. "Yes, that got rid of him and threw him off our scent."

Aunt Liz looked like she was ready to blow, I nudged her ribs with my elbow. She glanced down at where I was holding my abdomen. "The more urgent question," she stated, "is what the hell happened to you?"

I shoveled a few more spoonful's of soup into my mouth; I wanted to reduce the amount of soup I could lose when I told her. "The Principal and the Vampire Prince have secured my services to help them investigate several unusual deaths." Silence hung in the air. I took a deep breath. "Following the sheriff's visit we decided I should do this off the premises, so we went to the old abandoned hospital. After I'd examined the body," I threw a pointed look at Maggie. She didn't know what I could do. "It blew up."

Aunt Stella blinked. "Blew up?"

I nodded. "The hospital collapsed, but Hudson got to me in time and stopped the building from crushing me."

Aunt Stella's lips twitched. "The Principal saved your life?"

I rolled my eyes. "Don't romanticize it. He wants to figure out the weird shit going on, not date me."

Footsteps echoed down the hallway and we fell silent as Stephen Graham, the elderly vampire, stuck his head around the corner. He dropped his hat off his head and swept it down. "Good morning, ladies, myself and Mrs. Graham are ready to check out."

I glanced at Maggie. Get the hint, they want help. She beamed at him. "Great, would you like help?" Praise the good lord, she actually picked up on a social cue.

"I would be grateful, thank you, Maggie." She leapt up and slid her arm through his, leading him away from the kitchen.

Aunt Stella stood and closed the door. She spun towards me and crossed her arms, her cleavage enjoying the boost. "Spit it out, Cora."

"The shifters and vampires are being murdered by someone with magic. They have the ability to change form and possibly fool people as to their origins."

"They can change their scent?" Rebecca asked.

I shrugged. "The last shifter victim clearly believed he was a shifter, and the last vampire victim believed he was a vampire."

"That was the vampire that exploded?" Aunt Liz asked, her eyes assessing me. Dangerous Dave had nothing on my Aunt.

"Whoever is killing them knows my gift."

"How do you know?"

I stared into my Aunt's eyes. "Because he addressed me by name."

Everyone spoke at once, their voices whisper yelling in the small room. I scooped up the dregs of the soup and eyed the pan, calculating my chances of a second bowl. "Don't even think about it," Aunt Liz snapped. I sighed. "What did he say?" she asked.

"He predicted what I would think and held a conversation with me as if I was there." Apparently, I am that predictable. I glanced at Rebecca. "He came to the house a few nights ago."

Aunt Dayna leaned forward. "What?" I explained to them from beginning to end, starting with my first read on Daniel and finishing with me sitting here craving another bowl of soup. I left out my suspicions about Ric. Something didn't add up but I couldn't put my finger on it. My stomach rumbled on cue.

Aunt Liz sighed like the weight of the world sat on her shoulders. She slid from her seat, grabbing my bowl on her way, and ladled me another bowl of steamy soupy goodness.

I swear she added a little magic to it. She placed the bowl in front of me and squeezed my shoulder. "I'm surprised you are still standing after the week you've had. You must have burnt through thousands of calories and each time you do a read it takes a little something from you."

Stella leaned forward and scanned the women I trusted the most in this world. "Is anyone else concerned that the people who know about Cora's gift have expanded to include the Principal and his pet guard dog?"

My mouth was full, so I shrugged. Rebecca drummed her pretty pink manicured nails against the wooden table. They matched her sundress. A little wicked smirk tilted her lips. "There is a solution."

I swallowed the soup quickly to stop whatever crazy assed plan was about to leave her lips. "No."

She arched an eyebrow. Aunt Liz narrowed her eyes and glanced between us. "I'm listening."

"We draw him closer," Rebecca said, a small smile playing at her lips. Everyone leaned in closer.

I stood and grabbed my bowl, making my way to the sink. "How do you propose we do that?" Aunt Liz asked.

"Leave it to me," Rebecca said. I dropped the bowl, swiveled around and came face to face with Harry Forte. My mouth popped open. What in the hell? Harry Forte's soul should be laid to rest on House Forte's land. Why was he here? Did I fuck something up with my read? Maybe it was the bomb? But Sebastian would have known to take just one fragment of Harry back to be buried.

He waved his hand in front of my face; I blinked. Damn it. "You can see me?" he whispered.

"I'm going for a lie down, please don't set me up with the Principal. We can talk strategies later." I hurried out of the kitchen before they could make me agree to anything crazy. Harry glided along next to me.

"You can see me?" he asked again.

"Yes," I mumbled halfway up the first set of stairs.

"Why am I here? I know I'm dead, but I have been floating around White Castle like a paper bag in the wind. Then," he snapped his fingers in front of my face, "bam, a blinding light pulled me here."

I frowned. Blinding light? The soul stone, maybe? But that should have meant he ended up in my rooms. I pushed open my door and waited for him to come through before shutting and locking it.

"My name is Cora Roberts. You are dead, your blood was boiled until your organs turned liquid."

He staggered to my sofa and went to flop down. I grimaced a split second before... "What in the hell!" Harry shouted, rearing up and out of the sofa, literally. He stumbled forward through the coffee table and freaked himself out further. He backed himself into a corner, away from any furniture.

"You should be at your family's plot," I said, grabbing a Gatorade from the fridge. "Only loners without consecration come here."

His face fell. "Then why am I here?"

I shrugged. "You did blow up, maybe that has something to do with it?"

"Ric," he ground out. Harry's face hardened. "He did something to me after he murdered me."

"What?"

He ran a hand over his abdomen. "he put something in my stomach."

"A bomb."

He shook his head. "More like a psychic bomb," he glanced up and looked straight at me. "It was set to go off when it sensed your magic."

I frowned, I'd never heard of such a thing. I guess it was possible. Everyone had their own unique magical signature, and 'readers' existed.

"How long have you known Ric?" I asked, leaning against the kitchen counter.

Harry darted a look around the room, making sure Ric wasn't lurking in the bright sunlight. "A few weeks. He was the newest member of the group. Recently turned vegire." A slang word for vampires who refused to feed directly from people. Often because they'd made a mistake, taken too much. This meant Ric had posed as both a shifter and now a vampire.

"Did you know him before the group? I asked.

He shook his head. "No, he was new in town, no family, no friends. He was nice, brought snacks every time." If only we could all be judged on our snack dependability.

"Anything else you can tell me?"

He shrugged. "I'm dead, and I have no clue why."

He was dead to get to me. Harry worked this out the second I thought it. "You, he wants you. Why?"

Good question. Harry's face hardened. "I have no idea," I answered.

"You can speak to the dead. That's not exactly a common gift. Maybe he needs you for that."

"Once the dead move on, I can't speak to them. They don't come back and visit, you can't call them on the phone."

Harry frowned, then he stood straight. "Then I'll stay around until we bring him to justice."

Oh no, no no no. I could not add a ghost to the mix. "Thank you for the offer, but the afterlife should be calling you. It's where you can go to be in peace."

"I will not rest in peace until I bring Ric to justice. Until then, consider me your eyes and ears." He stood to attention and saluted me. Oh boy.

I managed a few hours of restless sleep, which accelerated my healing. As I descended the stairs, with a floating Harry to my left, Dave stood by the front door, arms crossed, staring Rebecca down. The Vampire Princess was amusing herself by decorating the area around Dave with balloons and banners. It was hard to look menacing with blue and silver balloons butting your head. I arched an eyebrow at Dave.

"Are you here to assist the decorators?" I asked.

"I'm here in case the murderer pays you a visit."

I rolled my eyes, pretended I couldn't see the crazy decorations destroying my house, and strolled to the kitchen. My heart sank to the floor at the sight of the empty stove. Aunt Liz's soup was gone. I grabbed the end of the loaf, sliced it in half and slid the two thick pieces into the toaster. Harry hovered around the kitchen. I worked on ignoring him.

Dave rounded the corner, making me jump. "Jesus, make a noise."

He smirked and strode straight through Harry. His lips dropped as death brushed against his soul.

Harry glared at Dave. "How rude."

Dave came to a stand next to me. The toast popped up, and I spun to butter it. Dave stared out the window at the makeshift graveyard. The sun was on its retreating path into the horizon, splashes of peach and orange coloring the cloudless sky.

"How many?" Dave asked.

"Twenty three."

His brows shot up. "Shifters?"

I shook my head. "No, bodies."

"Huh."

"So Hudson's 'thou shall not pee without my knowledge' declaration stands?"

"He's disturbed by these recent deaths. Until this week we were clueless. Then I bring you in and boom. Everything starts clicking together. The murderer ups his game, and he targets another faction. And all roads lead back to you. Why is that?"

I chomped on my buttery toast. Harry glared at Dave. "This man is questioning your morals. You put your life at risk, and he aims his suspicions at you. You should throw him out of your dwelling immediately." Only I could inherit a ghost with chivalrous tendencies.

"Am I a suspect?" I asked.

"You're a person of interest."

My lips tilted up. "Aw, you find me interesting."

Dave groaned, then snatched a piece of my toast. I scowled at him. "You want to hang out playing bodyguard, you'll need to bring a packed lunch. I don't feed shifters who consider me 'a person of interest'. I wouldn't want people to think I'm trying to bribe you."

"You're the bait." What an asshole.

Aunt Liz strolled into the kitchen, her eyes assessing GI Joe 2.0.

"And who might you be?" she asked.

"He's a pain in my ass," I supplied.

"He is a man of questionable ethics and should be promptly dis-invited to your home," Harry huffed.

Dave gave her his assessing stare. He'd catalogued everything from her eye color and bra size, to her build and likely strength. In return, Aunt Liz had his strength, ability and dangerousness pinned. She'd categorize him as a threat and treat him accordingly.

Dave crossed his arms. "Dave, head enforcer."

Aunt Liz retrieved a bottle of fresh pineapple juice from the fridge and three glasses. She filled each one and handed one to me and Dave. "Cora has her family here now, we can protect her. You are surplus to requirements."

"I'm not here to protect her."

"I'm bait," I supplied.

Aunt Liz stiffened. Declaring her niece as bait didn't endear him to my family.

"You can wait outside," Aunt Liz said, "this is a private family time, and you are intruding."

Dave gulped the juice, rinsed the glass and turned it upside down in the drainer. He nodded at me and slid out of the room.

"That was rude," I muttered.

Aunt Dayna bounced in, Maggie a step behind her. Oh joy, the calamity twins. Dayna grabbed my hand and pulled me out of the room towards the parlor. "Crystal ball, runes or tarot?" she asked, stopping at the sofa and plonking herself down.

"Runes," I mumbled, dropping opposite her and accepting the black velvet pouch.

I shuffled the runes around in the bag, concentrating on my general future. I selected three stones and dropped them onto the glass table. The dark green stones with gold etching peered back at us. Dayna's eyes went wide as she bent over them. "Love has eluded you for so long, but fear not, passion is on the horizon, but you will duel. If he is deemed worthy, then he will complete your soul." I refrained from rolling my eyes. It wasn't the first time Dayna had predicted undying love in my near future. But my liaisons remained brief and left a lingering emptiness, so much so, I'd stopped bothering. The last time was eighteen months, no, two years ago. It was like riding a bike though, right?

Maggie clapped her hands. "Time for the dress!"

This was the least favorite part of my birthday ritual. The night before, Rebecca, Maggie and Aunt Dayna presented me with three options for my party attire. Given that my wardrobe comprised of slacks and shorts, they took full advantage to get me out of my comfort zone and into something girly and, more often than not, sexy. Maggie tore from the room as Aunt Liz and Aunt Stella came and joined us for the show. Maggie bounced into the room with three bags. She handed the white one to Rebecca, the pale pink one to Aunt Dayna, and draped the black one across my lap. Oh boy, Maggie's choices were for her age, not mine. I unzipped the bag, preparing myself for slinky scraps of fabric. My eyebrows shot up as emerald green silk spilled from the bag. Wispy swaths of silk would wrap over my shoulders and crisscross down my back. I fingered the silk.

"Well? Do you like it?" Maggie grinned.

I nodded. "It's beautiful, Maggie." Her eyes lit up with the thought of victory.

Rebecca stood and peeled her bag apart. A floor length grey chiffon dress floated out. Gems adorned the lace bodice that glittered in the sunlight, sexy yet sophisticated.

Harry Forte floated into the room. "The shifter is still outside looking like a sniper without a rifle," he declared.

I glanced at him, then back at the dress. "I love it."

Harry frowned. "You love the shifter?"

"Wait, you've not seen mine yet!" Aunt Dayna said as she spun around to shield her bag. The sound of the zipper filled the room. The bag dropped to the floor and then she spun around holding a blue satin floor-length gown, the sleeves sweeping across the shoulders. It was simple and even more stunning for it. "You hate it," Aunt Dayna said with a tiny pout.

"No, I love them all."

Harry huffed. "They are dominant males, Cora, they won't share. You'll have to pick one, wanting them all is greedy." He strode through the sofa with his arms behind his back deep in thought, missing the fact I was talking about dresses and not declaring myself as a hussy for shifters.

Maggie took the dress from my lap, strode to the curtains and hooked it up on the pole. Rebecca and Aunt Dayna followed suit. For the first time all three of them had knocked it out of the park, and I seriously considered doing outfit changes.

"You need to choose one for your birthday, the others you can wear on dates with your true love," Aunt Dayna said pirouetting in the room.

"I can't decide, they are all beautiful."

Aunt Dayna continued to dance out of the room humming a tune. The front door creaked open, capturing the attention of the females in Summer Grove house. "Mr Dangerous," Aunt Dayna began. Save me now. "Would you be so kind as to offer your opinion as a male on Cora's dress?"

"I'm sure Dave has better things to do than look at dresses," I shouted.

"Yeah, like hanging outside like a creepy stalker," Aunt Stella mumbled.

"I'm sure you ladies can help her decide," Dave said.

Aunt Dayna stepped outside and behind Dave. She put her hands on his back and pushed him in the house. His eyes went wide as he caught my gaze. I hid a smile. You wanted to babysit a woman with a crazy set of aunts on a mission; you dug this hole for yourself, buddy.

Dayna directed him to the empty armchair. He dropped into it with a huff, his large frame dominating the furniture. He stared at the three dresses like they were enemies, I'd never seen him look so uncomfortable. Who knew that fabric would be the mighty Dangerous Dave's downfall?

"The green," he said.

I blinked. Harry paced in front of the dresses. "I agree, the green matches your eyes and will compliment your skin tone and hair color, plus the object of your affection likes it."

"Green it is," I declared, jumping up. "I have a few clients to catch up on."

"You need your beauty sleep," Aunt Stella called out.

"She needs to rest before the next body turns up," Dave interjected.

"Charming, you use her for bait and like a machine," Aunt Liz huffed. Oh boy, he was getting to my unflappable aunt.

"I'll get enough sleep to see to bodies and parties," I called out, traipsing down the stairs just as George, a regular guest and loner shifter, shot me a confused look. I shrugged. "I'm a doctor and it's my birthday tomorrow. The theme fits."

"Happy birthday, Cora," he said.

I rubbed my stomach, the flare of familiar phantom pain mixing with reality. The fuss might seem dramatic to some. But it was this or sink into the depression of memories that haunted me. Tomorrow would be the four-year anniversary of my worst nightmare. The crushing heartbreak had lessened over time, but the sting of betrayal lingered with brutal side effects. I blinked the tears back as I pushed into my office. Neil Crewdson may have once held my heart. In fact, I'd envisioned us married at this point—that was how much I loved him. He was safe until he wasn't.

CHAPTER THIRTEEN

Tiaras, capes, and beef wellington.

I ditched the mom bun and braids for a solid sheet of gleaming copper hair. Straightened, it touched the base of my spine. The green silk dress fit like a glove, even my breasts, which often tested my clothing, were swathed in fabric. I had a décolletage, but no porn star cleavage. I was dressed to the nines even though I was only going downstairs, not to a swanky restaurant. Gold strappy heels that were hidden by the dress added a few inches to my height, and my mother's emerald earrings dangled from my ears. I stepped out of my bedroom to find Harry sitting half on the sofa, his lap sunk beneath the cushions.

He glanced at me and shot to his feet. "Miss Roberts, you look outstanding."

Heat rose to my cheeks. Compliments from a ghost. This must be the pinnacle of my life.

"Shall we?" Harry announced, going for the door handle with his right hand and offering me his left. His hand swept straight through the handle. He sighed. "Does it get any better?"

"I don't know, all the ghosts I've met have passed on to their next life. Nobody has ever stuck around before."

He shook his head. "We need to catch the bastard that did this."

I stepped towards him, reached out and pulled my hand back. Now I was acting like an idiot. We both laughed.

My female friends and family greeted me downstairs, with the addition of Aunt Anita, who had piled her wild auburn hair onto the top of her head. She was Aunt Liz's non-identical twin. Her dark brown eyes sparkled with knowledge that eluded the rest of us. Aunt Anita was a Precog, the flip side to my gift. Aunt Dayna might dabble with the future, but if Aunt Anita told you something was going to happen, then in all likelihood, it would. The future depended on many variables and was therefore subject to change, but Aunt Anita got messages of the major kind and given that look in her eyes she'd seen something that amused her. She enveloped me with a hug. "You look beautiful, Cora," she whispered in my ear and then released me. I smiled and took in her lethal floor-length black gown, the slit reaching the top of her thigh.

"And you look dressed to kill," I said. In fact, everyone was dressed to kill. It had become a way to distance ourselves from the pain and bloodshed my birthday had suffered. Fake it 'til you make it, right? I plastered a smile on my face and tried to unburden my heart. The house smelled divine. Aunt Liz's cooking was always good, but when she pulled out the stops? Gordon Ramsay, eat your heart out.

"You look gorgeous," Maggie gushed.

"Elegant," Aunt Liz stated, flipping her hair.

We bustled into the formal dining room, the ten seater rectangular table laden with silverware and candles. I scanned the table twice and frowned. There were seven of us, Sebastian would be here soon, which would make eight. Why were all ten places set?

I opened my mouth to ask just as a clang echoed in my head. Visitors. Sebastian, I assumed. Aunt Dayna and Maggie shared a look. Right, expect the unexpected.

I strode to the front door and flung it open. I blinked twice at the enormous fist in my face and then into hazel eyes. He scanned me from head to toe and swallowed. *Who had invited the Terror of Tennessee to my birthday party?* I wondered as I glanced over his shoulder, seeing Dave smirking at me. *And the dangerous brooding sidekick to boot?* Hudson was clad in smart jeans and a white shirt. He looked... fucking lickable. Damn it.

"Can I help you?" I asked. If I play dumb, he might realize I don't want him invading my home.

"Happy birthday." He thrust a large pink box wrapped in a white ribbon and a bunch of flowers at me, beautiful pink peonies. "You look nice," he added. I accepted the gifts and stepped back with a sigh. My southern upbringing wouldn't allow me to turn him away. He strolled in, Dave entering on his heels dressed in his usual black outfit. I arched an eyebrow.

"No gift?" I enquired.

"Joint gift, except the candle, that was all him."

196

I closed the door and glanced over my shoulder. We had an audience. Even Harry was standing boggle-eyed at the two beasts. I jerked my head in their direction. "If you'd like to take a seat in the dining room?"

Dave strode towards them, Aunt Liz assessing his every move. I started down the hallway to the kitchen. The flowers needed water and distance. I needed distance, not the flowers. What were they thinking? A steady breath behind me made me pause halfway down the hall and spin on my heel. Hudson paused a foot from me. I waved the peonies at him. "I'm going to find a vase for my flowers."

"Are you going to open your gift?"

"Why? You stick one of those joke snakes that jump out and bite you in there?"

He smothered a laugh with his hand. I sighed and put the box and flowers on the sideboard, pulling at the satin ribbon which spilled to the side and popped the lid off. Copious amounts of pink tissue paper concealed a box of chocolate truffles and a plain white candle wrapped with a deep purple ribbon. I picked up the candle, curious why Dave had distanced himself from it.

"Thank you." I sniffed it and tried so hard not to screw up my face.

"It's a celebrities' favorite scent," he explained.

I glanced at the label, quickly put the candle down on the side table and put my hand up. "Excuse me just one moment," I said and spun towards the kitchen. Three seconds later I shoved my hands under the tap, threw on the scalding water and gave them a good scrub with the nail brush.

"What's up?" Rebecca asked, staring at my hands like they held my secrets.

I knocked the tap off, shook my hands and then grabbed a towel to complete the cleansing process. The front door creaked open and the familiar sound of Italian leather padded across the wooden floors. They paused. Oh crap. I dashed out of the kitchen, past a baffled looking Hudson and ran straight into Sebastian who was clutching the candle.

He smirked. "You bought one of these?"

The hairs on the back of my neck stood on end as Hudson moved behind me, silent like a predator. "It was a gift," Hudson said.

Sebastian's eyebrows hit his hairline before he bowed over and cackled like the three witches of Eastwick had possessed him. I glared at him in warning. Don't you do it.

"You bought her a candle that smells like some other woman's orgasm?"

He did it. I glanced at Hudson over my shoulder. I could see the heat struggling to sweep up his neck. "What? No." Hudson snatched the candle out of Sebastian's hand and read the label, something I'm certain he didn't do the first time. "I'll kill Dave."

Rebecca glided out of the kitchen with a vase, picking up the peonies and dropping them in the water. "Let's all take our seats in the dining room before Aunt Liz has an aneurysm." She ushered the three of us into the room, my usual seat at the head of the table being occupied by Dave. Sebastian nudged me. "You look amazing."

"Thank you."

Aunt Anita patted the seat next to her, a secret smile fixed on her lips. "I saved you a seat, Cora."

I plonked myself in the chair, Hudson occupying the seat to my other side. I slid a glance at Aunt Anita, well played aunt. Rebecca put my gifts from Hudson on the sideboard, the candle sitting innocently next to the chocolates.

Aunt Liz swept out of the room, the stiff satin of her silver gown pinning her body inside. I glanced at Dave whose eyes tracked her every move. He thought she was the biggest threat in the room. She was powerful, and could easily dump any shifter or vampire on their ass with a flick of her fingers. However, she wasn't the biggest threat in his midst.

I grabbed the pristine white linen napkin and unfolded it onto my lap. Aunt Dayna was holding an animated conversation with an intrigued Maggie and an amused Rebecca, something about her latest acting role. The rest of us sat in awkward silence, sipping our water and wine whilst we waited for the food to arrive.

"So, it's your birthday?" Dave asked.

I put down my glass. "Yes, it's not a Friday night ritual to get dressed up in silk and prance around the house."

"It should be," Hudson whispered low.

"How old are you?" Dave asked.

"Thirty."

He frowned. "That would mean you graduated as a doctor earlier than most."

"I excelled at my studies."

"She's one of the most intelligent women I've ever known," Sebastian added.

I glared at him. The vampires and shifters were behaving tonight; but I might not if he kept up this whole "wave Cora in the face of the shifters like a juicy steak" thing he's got going on.

Aunt Liz arrived with a cauldron of soup. She placed it at her space on the table and she began to ladle the light colored soup into the bowls, passing them along. The first one reached Dave, he stared at it like it was going to mutate and eat him instead. "What is this?" he mumbled to me.

"Pear and watercress, it's my favorite."

"No meat?" he asked.

I shook my head. "No."

"There better be meat in the main course, or I'm leaving. Who puts fruit in a soup?"

Aunt Liz's head snapped up, and she hit him with a cold stare. Oh boy. "You are here as a guest, not the main guest. In fact, if you left, no one would notice. I suggest if you want to continue to experience the hospitality of our host, Cora, you eat your soup and shut up."

Everyone but Aunt Liz, Hudson and Dave took a collective breath. "If you are going to fight, do it after the beef wellington," I stated, spooning some soup into my mouth.

Dave's features relaxed. "I apologize for my rudeness."

Aunt Liz placed the cauldron of soup on the sideboard and sat to eat her own meal. Something soft brushed against my ankle. I side eyed Hudson, who was eating his soup with obvious pleasure. I bent towards him and glanced between our seats, half expecting him to have grown a tail and for it to be wrapped around my ankle. Instead, startling blue eyes met me. The White Furry Menace sat on her haunches with a struggling mouse between her teeth. She blinked and dropped the mouse at Hudson's feet. You've got to be kidding. *It's my birthday you crazy feline and I still don't get the presents?* "Does she have a name?" Hudson asked. He was so close his breath brushed my cheek.

"Bella," I said, staring at her. She looked at Hudson and then wound her way between his legs. He reached down and ran a hand along her back. She arched her spine like a hussy and butted his hand afterwards.

"She likes her new name," he informs me, "but not her nickname."

"You channeling your inner Doctor Dolittle?"

He tilts his head up, his gaze snagging mine. "No, I'm good at reading anything. People, animals, witches…"

We got caught up in a stare off. "Pity you can't read this woman," I whispered.

"I'm reading you just fine, Cora."

"If you were then you wouldn't be looking at me like I was something you could ever have."

He grinned, all teeth. "Don't think yourself above me, little witch."

"Few people are above the mighty Principal, but this little witch won't ever be beneath you." I winked and turned back to my soup. My spoon paused at my mouth as I took in the silent table with eight people eyeing us with rapt attention.

"I picked a name for the cat, Bella," I announced. The feline in question shot out from under the table, hissed at poor Harry lurking in the doorway and slinked out of the room, tail in the air.

"I like it," Rebecca said, standing to collect the empty bowls. Dave had stuffed a non-protein food group into his mouth.

"So does she apparently," I muttered, handing her my bowl. "Wait." I bent down, picked up the mouse by its tail and deposited it in the empty soup bowl. Rebecca blinked, Hudson laughed. "It's just stunned, let it outside," I explained.

Maggie jumped up to join Rebecca and Aunt Liz as they made their way to the kitchen.

"So, Hudson," Sebastian began leaning back in his chair and studying him like an overbearing brother. Oh no, nope, not happening. "Do you have a girlfriend?"

"No," Hudson said.

"Mate?" Aunt Dayna asked, twisting to get in on this conversation.

"No."

"Boyfriend?" Aunt Stella asked.

Dave choked on the wine he was sipping. "No," Hudson answered, cocking an eyebrow.

"What's wrong with you?" Sebastian asked. I groaned and dropped my head in my hands.

"I'm picky," Hudson said.

"He's in between bed partners right now," Dave said.

I peeked between my fingers to see Dave grinning. "Would you like a girlfriend?" Aunt Dayna asked.

"No!" I shouted at the same time as Aunt Liz, who had entered the room with arms full of plates.

"But–" Aunt Dayna started by putting her hand up.

"No," Aunt Liz reiterated. "We are not discussing relationships at the dinner table; it's uncouth."

"Cora not getting any for years is uncouth," Sebastian mumbled.

I grabbed my fork and steak knife and attacked the beef. Sebastian's amused eyes met my glaring ones with a challenge. Funny man, he thought he had me cornered. I shoved a forkful of meat in my mouth and chewed whilst continuing the Sebastian stare off. If he wanted to air our private lives out in the open, then I would oblige. "You want to talk about love lives, let's discuss why I am your standing obligation date to your parents' monthly meals. Where is your Mrs. Vampire Charming?"

"The same place you left Mr. Elemental, baby," he said with a wink. I took a sip of wine and muttered a curse.

"Eat your steak and stop sticking your nose in my love life." Cora Roberts, master of the comeback, strikes again.

Dave is studying Rebecca with a slight snarl on his face. "What are you eating?"

"Nut roast," she explained.

He blinked. "You're a vegetarian vampire?" He said before swinging his gaze to me. "Only you could find friendship with the only vegetarian vampire in existence."

"It's a lifestyle choice, plus it keeps me looking young," Rebecca explained.

"You're a vampire, you are perpetually young," Dave muttered.

We finished up the main, the shifters devouring Aunt Liz's cooking with pleasure. Dave lifted his head after he'd cleaned his plate without licking it. "Liz, that was outstanding. You'll make someone an excellent mate one day."

"Unlikely, unless you have a praying mantis fantasy," Aunt Stella mumbled. Aunt Liz rolled her eyes as Maggie ran out of the room.

"Pass the plates," Aunt Liz said. We each passed our empty plates up to the head of the table. Then she took them and followed Maggie. A minute later the lights went out. The Terror of Tennessee stiffened next to me. I patted his leg. "Kitty afraid of the dark?" I whispered.

"No, I just don't like surprises."

"It's cake, there's no surprise."

Maggie rounded the corner, an enormous cake laden with bright candles in her hands. The happy birthday chorus began. Dave's deep baritone singing voice caught me off guard.

I blew out the candles and the lights came on.

"It's your favorite, carrot," Maggie said, sitting back down.

"Not chocolate?" Hudson said.

I opened my mouth to intervene but Aunt Dayna, quick to the party as always, blurted, "Cora hates chocolate."

Hudson glanced at the expensive chocolates on the sideboard. "She also has allergies," Sebastian announced with a smirk. I kicked his shin under the table, my heels helping to make it hurt.

Hudson ran his hand through his hair with a slight grimace. "In all fairness, it's not that I don't like flowers," I offered. Aunt Dayna jumps out of her seat and runs off.

Having her and Maggie in the house is more than I can handle.

"And if you're thinking of jewelry, I'll give you a tip," Sebastian said. Clearly I needed to kick him harder, and maybe higher. "Cora isn't your average woman, she appreciates those who take notice, who take the time to understand what she likes. She can't be wooed with diamonds and gold. Monetary value counts for nothing with Cora."

"I don't wish to be wooed by anybody, so this information is useless," I stated.

"Here we go, Princess," Aunt Dayna approached with her hands tucked behind her back.

"What now?" I asked. She whipped out a tiara with a wide grin.

"No, no, no." I shook my finger at her. "I'm one year too old for this birthday tradition."

Hudson raised a brow in amusement. "After watching Beauty and the Beast, a ten-year-old Cora declared she wanted to be a princess and have a beast marry her." They stare expectantly at Hudson for a beat. Wow. Subtle, my family was not.

"I think what she actually said was she wanted a castle like the Beast, and that Belle's crown was craptastic so she would need an upgrade."

"So we got her an upgrade." Aunt Stella pointed with her fork at the large tiara that barely even fit my head now.

I grab the tiara, plonk it on my head, and shove a strawberry from the side of the cake in my mouth. "You're all wrong. I said I wanted an enchanted castle with a talking candlestick and clock, and that Belle's color wasn't yellow, it washed her out, she should stick to blue. Oh, and that the Beast needed to grow up because freedom should be a given, not something to bargain her affections for."

"Wow, you were an articulate 10-year-old."

"I respect the hell out of Belle, she's the only princess to save her prince from a fate worse than death. She was no shrinking wallflower with a damsel in distress vibe that even as a ten year old pissed me off." I adjust my tiara to make sure it's not slanted.

"And you're adamant you don't have a savior complex?" Hudson says.

"I'm a doctor, not a hero."

"I'm also a doctor," Sebastian added.

Hudson looked between us. "That's how you met?"

I nodded. "We went to medical school together."

"All doctors have a god complex," Hudson said. Wow, that came a little too close to the mark.

I frowned. "I think you'll find doctors have an inherent need to help others."

He tilted his head towards Sebastian, who grinned as he said, "I was just bored, and I have a god complex."

I rolled my eyes just as the wards clanged in my mind. I winced. Not just someone, a multitude of someones. "What's wrong?" Hudson said.

I pushed my chair back and stood. "There's someone here."

The shifters and vampires stiffened. My aunts stood with me. Rebecca dashed to the window as I made my way to the door.

"What can you see?" I asked her.

She glanced at me. "Shadows. At least six, no, make it eight."

"Like the other night?"

She nodded. "They are sweeping the perimeter."

"It's more likely they are securing it," Hudson said, stepping next to me.

I frowned at him. "This is an attack on my home, you are a guest, you don't need to get involved."

"Here we go. Let me get your cape and tights." Ha-ha, superhero humor.

"I'll have you know many studies have declared capes are detrimental to the safety of superheroes."

"That so?"

I nodded.

"Then why the hell do you still keep getting hurt?"

Touché.

A wave of malicious power rolled through the house. My knees trembled, and I grabbed Hudson's arm to keep from collapsing. The sound of multiple bodies hitting the floor echoed around us. We glanced around before our eyes met. Just me and Hudson were left standing.

Chapter Fourteen

When the kitten is really a beast, show your throat or kiss

him.

"Cora Roberts I need to speak with you," a cold malevolent voice bellowed. I released my grip on Hudson's arm and twisted towards the door. He grabbed me around my waist.

"Release me," I hissed.

"Something unknown demands your presence after knocking out your family and friends and you run towards it?"

"I'm going to end the life of this fucker who dared to cross my boundaries and threaten my family. I'm going to make him suffer the way he made your shifters suffer. Boiling blood and terror will be the least of his problems."

His grip tightened as he drew me towards his body, his mouth dropped to my ear. "First rule of warfare, little witch, know your enemy. Do you know who or what he is?"

Silence stretched. "Not exactly."

"We shall discuss that minor revelation later, in the meantime you will not waltz to your death. He doesn't know I'm still standing. I'll go out the back and loop around. Wait one minute before you open that door." He released me and in the blink of an eye was out of the room and down the stairs.

I glanced at the grandfather clock and counted the seconds with the pendulum. The energy rolling through the property had a heavy ugly sticky feeling. It was stirring something primal inside me. I shuddered. If I let myself be free, the world would tremble in terror. Ten seconds. I approached the door and tore it open. I stopped on the porch inside my house ward as two shadows raced towards me and up the steps. They crashed into the ward; I gritted my teeth against the pain. They rammed into it twice more before retreating. Ric materialized halfway to the house as if

213

he stepped out of the shadows themselves, which was impossible. Whatever illusion he was pulling off, it was strong and would drain his magic. All good news for me. I reached out to the river, latching my magic onto the water in readiness. He grinned, spiky teeth on show just for me. Thanks for that nightmare. Shadows darted over my lawn.

Pausing at the bottom of the steps, he stared up at me from under his floppy brown hair. "Ric Nichols, what do you want?" I asked as I prepared myself to end the life of an elemental. Questions would be asked, I would have to appear before the Order. I needed to be sure he was the one committing these murders, and ideally the reason.

He lifted his arms out to the sides. "You."

I parked a hand on my hip. "There are easier ways of getting a girl's attention. Flowers, chocolates, a meal." The irony of that wasn't lost on me.

"I don't want to date you, Cora, I just need you to do your magic."

"My business hours are 8am to 6pm, Monday to Friday. Please make an appointment."

"I don't need a doctor, I need–" The boundary wards clanged again. Ric snarled and spun around. The shadows zoomed to him. Silent sentinels at his side. Was that Hudson? Heavy footsteps pounded up the driveway. Sheriff Robert Peterson came sliding to a halt on the gravel and whipped his gun out, aiming it at Ric.

"Police, put your hands in the air," he stated. He was calm and his hand steady as he faced down Ric. The shadows snuck towards him as he put his hands in the air. Oh no you don't. I yanked my magic to me. The water I stole from the river came rushing around the house, creating a barrier between the sheriff and Ric, trapping the shadows inside the water. I shot forward, my arm outstretched, ready to tunnel through the water. Ric grabbed my arm as I passed him, claws gouging from my wrist to my elbow. I screeched in pain, spun and slapped a thud of magic to Ric's temple that would knock anyone out. He shook his head and tightened his hold on me.

"You're strong, that's good. You'll need to be for what is to come," he growled.

"Not in this lifetime, buddy," I ground out as I slammed my knee into his groin.

He bent over, but his grip tightened. I glanced at the water barrier and found Sherriff Peterson fighting through it to get to me. The shadows were trying to claw their way to him, but they couldn't breach the barrier.

I tugged my arm, my warm blood seeping across our hands and onto the ground. I had a few minutes at most before I passed out. "Let me go."

His head snapped up, and I sucked in a breath. His eyes were the purest of black. It was like staring into the soul of death. The magical hit I'd given him and the water was draining me.

A roar straight out of prehistoric nightmares blasted us from the left. Ric was torn from me. A beast pinned him to the floor, his jaws reaching for his jugular. Ric smirked, winked at me and disappeared.

"Hudson?" I whispered. The magnificent, majestic beast spun towards me, fangs jutting out of his mouth. He was breathtaking. The world tilted sideways. Water soaked the floor as I landed on the ground and all went black.

"I demand to know exactly what is going on," a faint voice said. Masculine, familiar.

"When she wakes, we will discuss what to do with you," a gravelly voice declared. Dave.

"What do you mean do with me? I am the Sheriff of White Castle and you will tell me everything that is going on. The water, the shadowy things, the disappearing man and most disturbingly the beast you were before you turned back into whatever the hell you are."

"Cora?" Aunt Liz said from my right.

"Will she be okay?" Maggie asked.

"She'll be fine," Sebastian said. Someone stroked my arm. My brutally sliced open arm. I blinked my eyes open to find Sebastian's Nordic blue eyes studying me. He tucked a strand of dark hair behind his ear. "How do you feel?"

Sheriff Peterson leaned over the sofa I was laid on. "I'm okay, it was just a scratch."

I lifted my arm, finding it healed. If you squinted, there was a faint pink scar. I gripped Sebastian's hand. "Thank you."

He nodded. "Always."

I scrambled into a sitting position. We were in the parlor, my aunts spread out amongst the other supernaturals. They'd formed a protective circle around me. Each Aunt positioned to take out anyone who made a threatening move towards me. Maggie handed me a glass of orange juice, I accepted and gulped the contents in one go. She took the empty glass and replaced it with a full one.

"Well, that was one way to end a birthday celebration," I muttered.

Sheriff Peterson rounded the sofa and perched on the coffee table in front of me, his pad in one hand, pen in the other. He was dressed in pale blue jeans and a plain black T-shirt.

"Tell me everything," he stated.

I leaned forward and pushed the pad down. "Everything won't fit into a pad of paper. This information isn't to be written or shared. If we do this, you are accepting the terms that go with this knowledge."

A frown settled on his face. "Which are?"

"You will abide by the laws set out by each faction, you will disclose nothing to any other person. What happens on this side of the line isn't for the faint of heart. Last chance,

Robert, you can walk out of that door comfortable in the knowledge no laws were broken and nobody was harmed."

His gaze flicked to my arm. I turned it over to hide the scar. "Except you."

I shrugged. "Occupational hazard."

"You run a bed and breakfast."

I lifted my eyebrows. "What's it going to be, Robert?"

He placed the pad and pen on the table, and for a glorious second I thought he was going to choose the easy option and leave. "Hit me."

I glanced at Sebastian, then found Hudson leaning against the door frame. He gave a subtle nod. I launched into a brief explanation of the three factions, their existence and attributes. He took in the information with the calm stillness I've always associated with him. I glossed over what I do, but explained the shifter and vampire deaths.

"That's everything?" he asked.

"No, everything in terms of our history would take millennia to learn, our existence spans the same time that humans do. But you have the basics to police White Castle."

"So we need to catch this Ric?"

I shook my head. "No, you need to police the day-to-day problems of White Castle, call myself, Hudson or Sebastian if you encounter a problem you are unsure of."

"But the thing that is terrorizing the town is what I should concentrate on."

I resisted the urge to groan. "When he comes at you with shadows and claws, bullets won't stop him. When you are pinned to the ground by an unseen force, what will you do?"

He frowned. "I can help."

"Yes, by looking after White Castle and making sure the world keeps turning."

Sebastian placed a hand on his shoulder. "Leave this to us."

Robert shook his head. "Please, Rob," I said. "You are vulnerable. Everyone you see here has their own unique ability. They can fight this thing."

He stood and started pacing the floor. "I knew there was something freaky about this place." Here it comes, the freak out. He stopped and turned towards me. "Fine, I want to be kept in the loop though. If he attacks again or you get another body, I want to know."

I nodded. "Okay, deal." I put my glass on the table and stood. He stuck his hand out, and we shook.

He ran a hand over his shaved head and laughed. "I'll get going." He turned and took off out of the house. I nodded at Aunt Stella. "Please make sure he gets home okay. But take someone with you."

Aunt Stella grabbed Aunt Dayna by the arm and tugged her down the stairs towards the garage.

That left me with one ghost, two aunts, two vampires and three shifters. I glanced down at my gown. It was still immaculate. How I'd managed that I did not know, but I was grateful. The dress really was pretty.

"You think he'll keep his promise?" Hudson said, the rumble of his beast still close to the surface.

I eyed him with renewed curiosity. He wasn't just a shifter; he was a beast. I might have been out of it, but I was fairly certain in beast form, Hudson still towered over me.

"My aunts will bind him with a secrecy spell. If he tries to speak to anyone but us about what he knows, he will lose the memory."

"Eloquent," Dave said. "You are giving him a chance whilst mitigating the risk."

"We all know it's easier with the sheriff in the loop." I sighed. "It's late, can we reconvene to discuss next steps tomorrow?"

"Fine," Hudson growled.

Aunt Liz squeezed my arm. "Do you want us to stay longer?" she asked. I shook my head, this was my fight, and they had their own businesses and homes to take care of.

She smiled. "Okay, we'll be gone early in the morning, but we are only a call away."

"I made that potion you needed," Aunt Anita added.

"Thank you," I stated.

The aunts, Rebecca and Maggie made their way upstairs, tossing curious glances at Hudson and me. I gave Sebastian a quick hug who exited in a flash, leaving the front door open for the shifters to follow. They didn't move, so I started towards the stairs, passing Hudson by. I glanced up and found Maggie, Aunt Anita, and Rebecca hovering at the top of the stairs. They focused their wide eyes over my shoulder. I frowned and spun on the second step, finding Hudson directly behind me.

"What are you doing?" I asked.

"I'm staying."

I parked my hands on my hips. "No, I said we will discuss this tomorrow."

"And I said fine, but that doesn't mean I'm leaving you alone."

"And where do you think you are going to sleep?"

"Near you."

"Presumptuous asshole. A bunch of flowers, a box of chocolates and an orgasm candle won't get you into my bed."

"Orgasm candle?" Maggie said.

"I'll tell you later," Rebecca muttered.

"You have a dirty mind. This thing wants you, therefore where you go, I go," Hudson stated like it was a foregone conclusion.

"You are not entering my private apartment."

"Why, do you have dead bodies in there?"

"She keeps those in the basement, idiot," Rebecca stated. I shot her and the other two spectators a hard look. They scooted off to their rooms.

I rubbed my face with my hands. "If you are staying, you can take one of the unoccupied rooms on the floor below mine."

223

"You aren't powerful enough to protect yourself."

"Excuse me?"

"You might have water as an element. But your control was sloppy. If he turns up and you are alone, he will take you or kill you." I narrowed my gaze, Dave shifting in my periphery, his shoulders tensing. But I kept Hudson in my eyeline. Whereas Dave exuded menace and created a deep-seated need to run and hide, Hudson was a quiet coiled spring of power - you knew it was there, you tiptoed around it, trying not to disturb the beast and when you hit the trigger our primal brains would shout at us to make a futile choice - fleeing would incite the predator, freezing would prove you're worthless prey. If you were lucky, the beast would become bored and finish you quickly. If you weren't, then he would take you apart one agonizing limb at a time. I was obviously stupid, because my brain decided I should challenge the beast to a fight. Wrong f word brain!

Hudson carried on, either oblivious or uncaring to the insults he was hurling at me. "You lack control, you go in with your guns blazing without a plan or assessment of the danger."

I dropped my voice, low and dangerous. "I'm a medical doctor, I embody the very nature of control, assessment and planning."

"You wield your element like a blunt caveman tool - it's great for knocking someone over the head, but it lacks sophistication."

My hands fisted at my sides. "Really?"

"Really."

"Cora," Dave said, "whatever you are thinking of doing, don't." He thought I was going to hurt Hudson. That would prove his point. No, if he wanted control, I'd show him control.

I moved my hands in a clockwise direction evoking my magic and calling upon a specific body of water bending it to my will. The water lifted from the goldfish bowl, holding its shape as if it had been molded. Will and Kate swam oblivious to their predicament, their curious gazes taking in their new position. I pushed my right palm forward. Hudson took a few steps back down the stairs as the orb of water shifted and poised over his head. He glanced up, unimpressed. Yeah, yeah, I'm not finished yet. I twisted my left hand and swirled it anti-clockwise. The water expanded, and a hole appeared in the center, creating a donut of water with two bulging eyed goldfish. I lowered my hand so the ring of water settled around Hudson's face. I wasn't swirling the water; I was holding it in place.

Whilst power and force were to be feared, complete control over your element such as this was to be admired. It took practice and patience.

"Holy shit," Dave declared.

Hold your expletives, I'm not finished yet. I pried apart the ring and concentrated on creating a spiral that twisted around Hudson from his neck to his ankles. Will and Kate swam around him, uncaring that the Terror of Tennessee was their new guest. I let the magic flow, its pulse forcing the water to remain suspended. Finally, I gathered the water in front of me into an orb, and sent it back into the fishbowl. A gentle swish sent Kate and Will in a haphazard swim before it settled. Dave studied Hudson, then the floor. That's right, I had total control.

"Not one drop," Dave muttered as his eyes narrowed on me, assessing me as a threat to him, Hudson, the pack. Lord knows what rating he gave me. His features pinched as he tried to put things together. He wouldn't, he didn't have all the pieces.

"Do you show that amount of control in all areas of your life?" Hudson said, his voice low. The vibration did something to me. My heart skipped a beat and my breath picked up as I found myself snared in the trap of a beast far greater than Ric.

"Yes," I took a step backwards up the stairs, then another. Green rolled over Hudson's eyes. My foot paused on the next step.

"I think you'd like to demonstrate that to me."

I shook my head. "No."

"Your heart is beating twice as fast, your skin is flushed and your pretty green eyes are dilated. I bet if I kissed you right now, you'd melt."

My heart pitter pattered. In warning, or excitement? No, I couldn't like Hudson. "You're bluffing."

He stalked towards me; I resisted the urge to step back again. His eyes laughed at me. "Let's find out."

Dave went preternaturally still. Hudson chuckled. Oh boy.

"I don't bluff. You'll learn." I held still.

"Hudson?" Dave said, low like he was trying not to disturb the beast.

"Leave us," Hudson growled. No, don't leave us!

Dave sighed and walked into the parlor. I blinked. "Where is he going?" I whispered.

Hudson prowled up the stairs towards me, I took a step back for every one he took forward. "He's giving us space to work this out."

"Work what out?" My foot hit air, and I stumbled backwards. Hudson lunged forward and captured me around my waist. He backed me into the wall and caged me in with his arms. His spicy woodsy scent invaded my senses. He ran his nose from my ear, down my throat and along my bare shoulder. I stayed still. Maybe he'd get bored and leave me the hell alone.

"Do you accept the bet?" I shook my head. If he kissed me now, after several brushes with death, I'd probably throw caution to the wind and drag him upstairs. That's it. This was some weird survivor's attraction.

He leaned back and tilted his head. "Am I not good enough to bet with? You bet the bloodsucker?"

228

"The bloodsucker is a friend, someone I trust. You are dangerous."

A slow smile crept across his face. "You're scared."

"No, I'm intelligent."

"You're scared that you'll enjoy it. You want me, but you fear letting your guard down long enough to expose yourself."

That hit a little close to home. "You will not manipulate me. You want me, you woo me."

"What is this, the 1920s? Who says woo?"

"This is me explaining to a kitten that he can't have this toy."

"You're refusing me?"

I lifted my arms. "Praise the lord, I got through to his holiness."

He leaned in so close, you'd struggle to slide a sheet of paper between us. I tipped my head back as I stared into his eyes. I didn't flinch at the full on alpha stare he leveled at me, and my eyes definitely didn't drop to his lips, stretched into a wicked smile. He would be the death of me.

"Why?" he growled.

"You collect women like someone else collects stamps," I whispered. "Once you've licked it and stuck it in, you forget all about it."

"Cora, if I lick you, I'll own you. The only place you'll be going is my bed."

"I'm not sleeping with you."

"Who said anything about sleeping?"

I rolled my eyes. He closed in, his lips a hair's breadth from mine, his hard chest brushed against mine causing delicious little tingles to run down my spine. I licked my lips and glanced at his again. I shut my eyes and took a breath.

"No," I whispered.

"Who did this to you? Who put the fear of passion in your eyes?"

"Nobody."

"You're lying."

I pushed on his chest. He didn't budge an inch; it was like pushing against concrete.

"I've known you all of five minutes. I don't trust you."

The third door to the left opens and Rebecca glides out, her eyes widening as she takes us in. My god, what must we look like? Me pinned to the wall by the Terror of Tennessee.

"Cora? My television is acting up again. Could you help, please?" She blinked, a picture of innocence.

"This conversation isn't over," Hudson growled into my ear. Goosebumps broke out down my arms. It was said like a sensual threat. I had a weakness for capable males. Ones that made me feel like I might be safe in their arms. Hudson was my ultimate weakness. The problem was, those males also had the capacity to gut you. So I stayed out of their lane and in mine, passing liaisons with males I needed to watch my strength with. It often left me feeling unfeminine and unsatisfied. But it was my choice, and it kept me safe.

Hudson stepped back, I turned and hightailed it past Rebecca and into her room, the one with no television.

CHAPTER FIFTEEN

Politics, princesses and principals.

Meals with vampire royalty called for dresses, decorum and a delightful disposition that I could pull off once a month. Luckily my obligations to Sebastian were just that, once a month. He was, by their own laws, bound to present a suitable mate to his parents at these meals. Nowhere in these laws had anyone indicated that this mate should be a vampire because no one had ever dared to turn up with anyone but a vampire before now. The ruse we provided was one of a long courtship, I was a doctor and of a strong elemental bloodline. No one could argue I wasn't a suitable mate, I just wasn't the right species.

I arrived downstairs in my new grey chiffon gown at 7:30pm to find Dave hovering around the front door. He'd spent the day helping me with chores. I'd learnt he was terrible with a paintbrush, but handy with a screwdriver. The cupboards in the kitchen now hung straight and the shelves in my office were also level for the first time.

The door opened and Sebastian swanned in. He glanced at Dave, took in his black attire and frowned. "Did you go home last night?" he asked.

Dave glanced at me and smirked. "I did, Hudson spent the night."

I rolled my eyes and groaned. "In one of the guest rooms. You are a worse gossip than the church knitting group."

He grinned. "I'm their mascot."

Huh, Dangerous Dave had a sense of humor. Who knew?

"You look stunning," Sebastian said, offering me his arm. I linked it and glanced over my shoulder at Dave.

"I'll be back in a few hours. Take room six on the second floor." I'd given up trying to make them feel uncomfortable, to get them to leave. Dave's lips tilted up, I frowned. Dangerous Dave smiling wasn't a good thing.

I closed the door and descended the steps with Sebastian. Puffs of white back-lit with coral from the descending sun dotted the Louisiana sky. I paused and blinked at the fancy red Ferrari. "You got a new car?"

He opened the passenger door and shrugged. "I keep losing my baby to you, so I thought it was time I had a backup. I can't keep driving around in my suped up Mom carrier."

I folded myself into the leather seat. The door closed with a thud. He rounded the car and was spinning the Ferrari out of the drive in seconds. "You could just stop betting me."

He glanced at me as he pulled onto the main road and let the engine loose. "Where would the fun in that be?"

"Anything I need to know about tonight?" I asked. It wasn't unusual for Sebastian's father to blindside me with topics of conversation I should know about had Sebastian and I actually been dating. The last one was regarding a birthmark Sebastian had on an intimate part of his body. I'd blushed like a virgin on her wedding night as we discussed that topic.

He shook his head. "Anything I need to know about last night?"

I smoothed my dress. I think it came joint favorite with the green silk. "Hudson made a pass at me."

"And?"

"And I told him no."

"Huh."

"What?" I snapped.

"You told him no?"

"That's right."

"But he's your type. Strong, alpha male, calm, attractive in a rugged way."

"Exactly."

"I'm not following."

"He's exactly my type. So let's run this through. I say yes, we sleep together maybe a few times. I begin to fall for him. I see a future with him. Now it goes one of two ways; either we continue our relationship, but because he's the Principal, he would demand that I live in the pack and govern by his side. If we actually marry or mate, it would mean I would give him access to my power and potentially lose it."

Sebastian's lips twitched. "Or?"

"Or, the more likely outcome, we sleep together, I fall for him, then he gets bored and moves on to his next challenge, leaving me with a broken heart and an even more bitter attitude towards relationships."

"You've got this all figured out."

"I have."

"He isn't Neil."

The trees outside the car blurred through the lens of my tears. "I'm aware."

We rode in silence the rest of the journey to Castle Elliot. That's right... Sebastian's parents, the king and queen, lived in a medieval-style castle, grey stone and turrets galore. It was a little gaudy for my tastes and lived up to the gothic expectation associated with vampires. We trotted up the thirteen steps as Frances, the Elliot's chief butler, opened the arched wooden doors. He glanced at me with disdain before bowing; I resisted the urge to roll my eyes. Frances was old school. He believed vampires were above the rest of society and they shouldn't mingle with the riff-raff.

"Master Elliot, your parents are in the drawing room awaiting your arrival."

Sebastian nodded and dismissed Frances, who shuffled off towards the kitchen. We stood in the open doorway.

Sebastian linked his hand with mine. "Maybe it's time you took a chance," he said before frowning and staring out of the open door into the gardens.

"He would have to be extraordinary to take that risk. I'm not sure Hudson fits the bill," I whispered. Sebastian's parents weren't dumb. They knew this was a ruse so that their son didn't have to spend his time courting vampires. They tolerated me. Queen Aira was kind and accommodating, King Leon needed a kick in the nuts.

"It seems you are going to be checking out that theory sooner rather than later," Sebastian muttered.

I followed his gaze as a tall, imposing figure ducked under the arches of blossoming yellow roses. I blinked. What the hell was he doing here? Trespassing on royal vampire territory by the Principal would be seen as an act of war. That's the last thing we need. Hudson glanced up and met my eyes as he started up the steps. "Extraordinary? I can manage that," he growled at me. Wow, I'd pissed off the

Principal when he was half a mile from me. How had he even heard that? *Cora Roberts—master of inserting one's foot into one's mouth.*

"What are you doing here?" I asked.

"I invited him," Leon Elliot declared. I twisted my head as he and Aira glided down the spacious stone hallway over the oriental silk rugs. They were too pretty, too perfect, all sharp cheekbones and glossy hair. Sebastian inherited his dark hair from his father, but Leon styled his short. Aira was classically beautiful, with peaches and cream skin, wide eyes and full lips. Her chestnut hair was pinned back. Between them they had lived over five hundred years on this planet. I couldn't even fathom the knowledge they had and events they'd witnessed. Neither looked a day over thirty.

Leon had a wicked gleam in his eye that I saw in Sebastian when he was plotting something. I frowned as Leon passed me and held out his hand to Hudson. They shook. "Welcome to my home," Leon said. He was as cold as always.

Hudson took Aira's outstretched hand and kissed it, as was the custom. "Thank you for your kind invitation to share a meal," he drawled. Look at that. The beast had perfect manners. I wondered if they knew what he shifted into? I'd pegged him as a cat, but I would have guessed a lion. Not a prehistoric overgrown monster that was taller than me, with jaws that stretched wide enough to eat a person... whole. I suppressed a shudder. Sebastian's hand landed on the base of my spine and we started towards the dining room. Apparently the bloodsuckers had invited the beast to dine with us. These normally dull evenings had shifted to being a political minefield.

We rounded the corner into the informal dining room. This held a glass table which seated six in high-backed chairs. A woman stood from the dining table. She was tall with a blonde pixie cut that accentuated her already sharp cheekbones. Her big blue eyes blinked at Hudson. She hid a coy smile. Dressed in white, she looked like a lamb being brought to slaughter. Oh boy, this was a setup.

King Leon waved his hand at her. "Hudson, meet Ivy, she's the Princess of Switzerland and is hoping to form strong links in America." Leon glanced at Sebastian, whose face had gone blank.

Hudson kissed her outstretched hand. "Pleased to meet you."

She blinked eyelashes that could fan the warmest room in Louisiana. "This is Cora Roberts, my son's…" Leon gritted his teeth, "partner."

Hudson's eyebrows snapped together, I gave him a subtle shake of my head as I stuck out my hand. I wasn't kissing anyone's hand, whether they slept on a hundred mattresses or on the street. "Nice to meet you. How long do you plan to stay in America?"

Okay, so it came out bitchy. Her eyes shot to Hudson, then to Sebastian. Hmm. "I plan on being here as long as it takes to secure a union between our countries." Her tone made me itch. It was said as if she could come and pluck any male from my country for her own. She was as sinful as Rebecca, only difference, Rebecca didn't hide it.

King Leon smiled as he took the seat at the head of the table. I moved to his left, one chair down, Sebastian went to sit across from me, which would be next to Ivy. Hudson moved to my side.

"No, son, sit next to Cora today. Hudson can keep the lovely Ivy company."

Ivy sat, Sebastian rolled his eyes and Hudson froze like one of Madame Tussauds figures. Aira sat at the opposite

240

end of the table and plucked her napkin from her plate. She blinked at the three of us. Was Leon trying to set Ivy up with Hudson? It would strengthen the relationships between their factions. I sat, Sebastian swapping sides with Hudson, who sat opposite me. Somebody's foot smacked my knee. I snapped my head up to Hudson. He grinned. "Sorry, Cora, I have long legs and big feet."

Sebastian sighed like this was the worst night of his life and mumbled, "I suppose we are to assume you are alluding to the mythical relationship between your foot length and your co–"

"Sebastian Elliot!" Aira shouted. I blinked, she never lost her temper. Well, this shindig was off to an unusually colorful start. Maybe for the encore Maggie could invite everyone to the singles evening?

"Sorry, mother."

Servers appeared and placed some kind of salad before us. Good thing Hudson left Dave at my house.

"Have you been courting long?" Ivy asked, taking a dainty bite of an orange slice. You don't need to nibble an orange segment, the food is already broken up for you. What was she, a bird?

Sebastian clutched my hand, the one white knuckling the knife. He rubbed his thumb over my knuckles. "Cora and I have been dating for years."

Her eyebrows shot up. "But you haven't mated? Why?"

Hudson smirked as he polished off his salad. His eyes were laughing at me. "We are happy, we don't want to rush things," I answered.

"Is it because he could take all your power?" she asked.

I stabbed some rocket leaves. "Why would he do that?"

Ivy frowned. A tiny knitting of her brows that made her look like a cute puppy. Apparently, I wanted to stab cute puppies. "Well, in the mating of elementals I believe the male can call upon the power of the female and often drain her of her power completely."

I took a hearty sip of my crisp white wine. One thing the Elliot's had was a good wine cellar. "The power share between elementals is not completely understood, and in the union where the female is much stronger than the male, it has been known to go the other way."

Ivy chuckled. "Are you suggesting you are more powerful than the Crown Prince of America?"

Sebastian's hand tightened on mine. It was a warning. Lie. "Of course not. I'm just correcting a misconception that continues to plague our faction."

"What happens if the female is more powerful?" Ivy asked.

I shrugged. "Then the female can drain the male's power."

Everyone froze as the servers materialized through the four doors in the corners of the room and took our plates away, before replacing them with a soup. Oh boy, we were here for the tasting menu. The first three months were like this, course after course, whilst Leon picked me apart. By month four we were down to four courses, and this last year two courses; main and dessert.

"So you need to find someone weaker than yourself," Ivy pushed. "Sebastian is royalty."

I put my spoon down with a clatter and looked at her. "And?"

"And, you are out of your league."

"Father, please control the mouth of our guest, the standards for social occasions must be of a lower standard in Switzerland."

243

Leon coughed around his soup. Ivy had the brains to blush. But it was calculated. She touched Hudson's forearm with a sly glance at me. A flare of something hot shot from my stomach to the back of my throat. No… nope. I could not be jealous. What was happening?

"I need a little air before the next course. Would you accompany me outside in the gardens?" she asked as if the gardens might hold attackers that would threaten her non-existent virtue.

"Of course," Hudson said. It was mechanical. There was no fire, no growl, no passion behind his words. With me, he made words feel like foreplay. I offered them a polite smile as she pulled him through the door closest to the outside. It clicked closed. Then Sebastian rounded on his father.

"What is the meaning of this? I met her and said no."

I blinked. They met? When? "She might have spoken out of turn, but she was correct. Cora is below you. Ivy is suited to your station."

"Or species," I mumbled. Because beyond this facade was the simple fact. They didn't like me because I was an elemental.

"Ivy is a manipulative bitch with her eyes set on being queen of the most powerful country in the world."

Leon slammed his hand down. "And Cora is a backward town doctor with a spit of magic, she is below you son."

"Say what you really think," I added. If he knew what I was, he might be the first vampire to die of a natural heart attack.

"I know what you do and I don't agree with it. The rites of passage you perform for other factions are overstepping the mark."

He could pick on my faction, my upbringing and even my intelligence. But he was not making me responsible for the errors of his own race. The door opened just as I spun in my seat to face Leon completely.

"Do not lay at my door the faults in your own factions. Without me those people would wander the earth lost. If they don't follow *your* rules, they don't go to the promised land. Do you know what they call that in the human world?"

"Religion," Leon spat.

"Wrong." I punctuated my words by stabbing my finger on the table. "It's a cult. In most human religions you don't have to go bowing every Sunday in the house of god. Their god welcomes you with open arms, if you have faith He is there."

"They are a sloppy race with loose morals," Leon ground out.

"Yet they outnumber ours ten to one, and their faith is a powerful force that outstrips yours. You may have centuries of knowledge, but you don't use it to fuel your understanding. You use it to fuel your ignorance, you pick on the events that support and strengthen your own beliefs. Try getting off your high horse and go visit your own species. Speak to your subjects, don't lord over them, be a voice for them in this world. Fight for what they need. Be their champion, not their executioner."

"Be careful, Miss. Roberts, you are treading close to treason."

I rolled my eyes just as Hudson and Ivy came back into the room. Hudson's face was blank, whilst Ivy wore a pout. "You are not my king, therefore I cannot commit treason against you."

"I should report you to the Order," he ground out.

"Leon," Aira said, her soft voice floating between our angry auras. We both looked at her. "Maybe she has a point?"

Leon scoffed, plucked his napkin from his lap and slammed it down in front of him. "The day I listen to a woman nicknamed 'The Undertaker' about politics will be the day hell freezes over."

"Our factions aren't perfect," Hudson said, taking the seat opposite me.

I glared at him. "I didn't ask for your help."

He arched a brow. Ivy looked like she wanted to melt into the soup. "No, but you need it."

I pushed my chair back and turned to Aira. "Excuse me, I don't feel well so I will leave to go to my ramshackle house in my backward home town." Aira sighed as I made my escape. My fingers curled around the handle of the front door when someone caught my arm. I swung around, ready to smack the culprit. I hated being grabbed. Hudson ducked and laughed.

"Let me go," I muttered. He backed me out of the front door and shut it behind us, keeping one hand on my wrist. I donned my bored expression even as the hair on the back of my neck lifted and my stomach quivered. He backed me into a corner of the porch and pinned my wrist above my head. I wrestled with the need to flatten him to the floor and escape. He leaned against me, pinning me to the wall.

"No, you need to calm down. How many years have you been coming to these meals and kept your cool?"

"Four," I gritted out.

He leaned in further, crushing me to his hard body, and ran his nose along my collarbone and up my neck. My heart tripped, and fever spilled into my veins. I suppressed a shiver. Mayday people, mayday. Where the hell was Sebastian?

"So the bloodsucker invites me the day after I come to your party and sets me up with a Vampire Princess. He did it to get to you."

"Why would you dating a vampire princess get to me?" I whispered.

He smiled against the sensitive skin under my ear. "You like me."

"I tolerate you."

"You like me, you want to kiss me."

I did, I really, really did. Kissing him would be an experience. It would be full of strength and passion, it would be a sweet release giving my heart a high. I wouldn't have to hold back... much. I could let lose my magic and not worry about the consequences. He could handle it. The attractiveness of that was dangerous and intoxicating. "Full of yourself, aren't you?"

He pulled back, his alpha stare in full force as his nose brushed mine. Every part of him was focused on every part of me. It was intimate in a way that unsteadied my soul. He gazed at me as the seconds ticked by. My eyes stung from not blinking. He inched forward and licked his full lips. My palm landed on his left cheek, the smack echoing around the porch.

"What was that for?" he growled.

"You were going to kiss me."

"A simple no would have sufficed. I don't force myself where I'm not wanted."

"I told you no."

"When?"

"I…" Shit, no I hadn't. I just daydreamed about his lips. *Idiot.* "This is the second time in twenty-four hours you have offered yourself to me on a plate, and it is the second time I am telling you no. Next time I won't be so polite."

He blinked, the smile never leaving his lips. I was fooling nobody, least of all the beast that could probably scent my lies. "Cora, kiss me, I dare you."

I pushed on his chest. "I'm not ten years old, daring me won't get you what you want."

"What will?"

"I already told you."

"You want the flowers and chocolates. You want the mating dance?"

An image of him naked, dancing around me like some weird bird hit me. I frowned. "No."

He pulled back, giving me space. "What then?"

"I want the world. I want the man who sweeps me off my feet to be loyal, not waiting for the next model. Younger, fitter, more beautiful. I want to lose myself and know I am safe. I want him to be my intellectual equal, he needs to be able to handle my strength and not be terrified by it. I want someone who will accept all my faults and sins and not try to change me."

"You want prince charming."

I shrugged. "I want extraordinary, nothing less." He sighed and stepped back. "I need to get home." He nodded and dug in his pocket, pulling out a key. He pointed it at the Ferrari. "Why do you have the key to Sebastian's car?"

He trotted down the stairs and opened the passenger door. "He asked me to take you home, something about sorting out some family issues."

I followed and slid into the car. The ride home was completed in silence. When he exited the car and followed me into my home, I didn't protest. Dave shot us both a weird look as he passed us on the way out the door. "All quiet here," Dave stated.

"Given the killer's infatuation with Cora, I'm sure it won't remain that way. I'll be staying tonight."

"How did the meal with the royal bloodsuckers go?" Dave asked.

He knew? Of course he did. I trudged up the stairs to my room as Hudson's voice floated upstairs.

"Goodnight, Cora, have extraordinary sweet dreams."

CHAPTER SIXTEEN

Come creeping in the middle of the night and expect a

war cry from the bowels of hell.

I was in the zone between dream and reality when the floorboards outside of my bedroom creaked. My brain snapped awake, and I steadied my breath as I ran scenarios from sleepwalking guests to murderous vampires. My shotgun was downstairs. Clever thinking Cora, because logically the wards shouldn't let anyone in the house who meant harm. But there were always exceptions. No ward was infallible. Whatever their intentions, if they came uninvited creeping into someone's bedroom, they deserved whatever happened to them. Even human laws protected you from that.

A shiver danced through my body as adrenaline flooded my veins in fiery warning. I stayed perfectly still as the handle on the door squeaked at being turned the wrong way. My aunt had put it on backwards years ago after decorating.

Whoever was on the other side of that door wasn't familiar with the house.

I was lying on my belly, ass out in the air for all to see, my bumblebee panties giving anyone who saw them the advice to 'bee happy'. I'm sure I looked about as lethal as a caterpillar. My hair was hanging over my face, allowing me to squint at the door as it opened. A colossal figure cloaked in shadow loomed on the threshold. My heart jack hammered in my chest like it was trying to up and leave me. Tough shit you coward - where I go, you go. The missed beats suggested it was flipping me off whilst packing its bags. The figure stepped into the room, their head turning from side to side to examine their surroundings. That's right, motherfucker, I'm fast asleep, you take your time deciding how to end my life. They edged closer to the bed. They were enormous. The only chance I had was surprise.

They took the final step. With a war cry, I shot from the bed in a ball of fury, flinging myself at them. They staggered back before grabbing my fists inches before a throat punch would have put them down. I thrust my knee up; I was sure they were male, so I prepared to rob him of his ability to create life.

He twisted and caught my leg in his other hand twisting it across his body leaving me hopping on one foot.

My head slammed forward. A broken nose should dislodge him. He leaned back enough that all I did was headbutt his chest. For the love of...

"Let me go," I growled.

"Such a delightfully violent little witch."

Hudson. The conceited, arrogant, asshole.

"Why are you in my bedroom?"

"I came to tell you something."

"Ever heard of this little communication device, that's all the rage now? You punch numbers into it and then it connects you to the person you want to talk to?"

He chuckled. "I tried calling, four times."

I frowned, still hopping on one foot whilst he held me like a disobedient child.

"I must have passed out," I mumbled. "Let me go."

In the dark, I could make out the outline of his features. He cocked his head. "Are you going to behave?"

I tutted. "I always behave, you're the one sneaking around in the dead of night like a creepy stalker."

He relaxed his grip on me, briefly holding me in place before releasing me. I turned, hammered a kick to the back of his knee and went to drive my elbow into his thick skull. Hopefully, it would teach him a lesson.

He grunted, his leg buckling slightly. I had given everything I had in that kick. What was he made of? Concrete?

His arms swept around me as he took me to the ground. His hands cupped my head as we hit the floorboards. I huffed out a breath as he pinned my wrists above my head and he squeezed his legs around the outside of my thighs, trapping me. Game over, Cora.

"Now what are you going to do?" he asked.

Erm? He bent down, his breath tickling my ear. I suppressed the shiver tightening my spine and glared at the ceiling. My heart was unpacking its bags and grabbing the popcorn. "You too chicken to fight me, witch?"

Fuck it. I snapped my head to the side. His stubble grazed my cheek as I faced him. I tilted up, capturing his firm lips in a kiss. Within two seconds, they'd caved and opened up to let me in. The taste of him was purely masculine and totally, Hudson. Wild and untamable. Sunshine and storms. Our tongues tangled as the battle for dominance played out across our bodies. I lifted my hips. He growled into my mouth. I experienced a flush of feminine satisfaction at making this beast growl for me.

The kiss deepened until oxygen became a secondary concern. It was bliss. He rolled us, leaving me straddling him. One hand travelled under my T-shirt and up my spine. The other tangled in my hair, controlling my head so I couldn't escape his kiss. I crumpled against him. I was falling and I couldn't bring myself to care. It had been so long since someone kissed me with a passion like this. Scratch that, nobody had ever kissed me like this. Like I was their world. He tugged on my hair, arching my neck and baring my throat for his lips to paint a hot path down to my breasts. We were about to have sex on my bedroom floor.

"Hudson," I whispered. His hands cupped my ass, and he stood, taking me with him. My back landed on the bed a second later, his hands pushing up my T-shirt to expose my breasts. He placed open-mouthed kisses on the sensitive underside of both breasts, the building pressure in my entire body making me jittery with anticipation. He licked along my scars, the flesh sensitive. I sunk my hands into his hair and tugged him towards my nipple. His hands shot out and grabbed mine, pinning them above my head. My fingers clawed the sheets as I fought to maintain some solid ground. His mouth landed on my nipple and sharp teeth scraped the outside. My eyes shot open in confusion. He had fangs? I opened my mouth to protest, then he sucked. My back arched, and I wrapped my legs around him. A moan rolled out of my mouth and my magic splashed across the room. The windows rattled with the power, and I reeled it back, just. This wanton sex goddess could not be me. I was always in control, my bedmates were weaker than me, easily overcome and easy to walk away from afterwards. Hudson was destroying me with a kiss. Women didn't walk away from him, they crawled after he'd destroyed them, one stroke of his lips at a time. I couldn't let that be me. He ground against me. Lust flooded my body. Jesus Christ, what was he packing down there? He worked down my body one agonizing kiss at a time. My phone started ringing. Go away… we ignored it as he worked his way across the lace band of my panties.

"Don't tease," I said.

He laughed against my stomach. "You walk around like a siren, tempting the most virtuous man to sin and taste like an angel, yet it's me teasing you?"

His words froze the heat in my veins. "Let me go," I mumbled.

He came further up my body, his full on alpha stare studying me. Flecks of amber swirled as he frowned. "What just happened?"

"You reminded me why I would never do this with you."

He leaned back and released my hands. I pushed my T-shirt down just as Harry floated through the wall. He looked between me and Hudson. "Miss Cora, I thought I should give you fair warning you have another gentlemen visitor." His eyes widened at Hudson.

"Enlighten me," Hudson growled as I wiggled free and swung my legs off the bed. I grabbed a pair of jeans and threw my legs into them.

I spun to face him as he climbed off the bed. His hair stuck out at odd angles where I'd pulled on it.

"You want a tumble in the sheets, bed the little witch to pass the time whilst we hunt this killer. You want someone to warm your bed whilst you can't be amongst your own kind. I'm sure there's a nice shifter waiting for you back at the pack house."

I opened my bedroom door just as Sebastian opened my apartment one. I glanced at the clock above the sofa, 6am. Why was my home filling with the elite of the factions at this ungodly hour? Hudson stepped out behind me, Sebastian's eyes widened. Right, he would take some convincing that we hadn't just had wild monkey sex.

"You want to know what I think?" Hudson growled out. Great, I'd pissed the Terror of Tennessee off.

I spun around to face him. "Not particularly, but you live to hear your own voice so you are probably going to tell me."

He tilted his head down to stare at me. "People cheat. You need to move on and stop letting it rule your life."

Furious fiery rage flooded my senses and nausea churned in my stomach at the memories being shoved in my face.

Sebastian sighed. "Bad move man, bringing up the ex-boyfriend."

I tilted my head to the side, forced myself to maintain eye contact and locked my emotions down tight. "You think you know me?" I whispered.

"Avoiding men you could actually have a future with is a classic of the scorned lover. It's not unique and people move on."

"You're right, it's a classic, but in this case, you are wrong."

"Then what? He left you with a Dear John letter?"

I turned on my heel, stalked past Sebastian and out of the door. I wasn't having them sully my only place of peace on this Earth. Well, that and the graveyard.

"Leave it alone," Sebastian advised.

The long existing betrayal that had sunk its claws into my heart flared. I stuffed it back into its box and shoved it to the furthest corner of my brain. Neil Crewdson had had enough of my tears and pain.

Footsteps padded behind me as I trotted down the stairs. "Running again?" Hudson growled out. "Shit gets real and you bail."

I found myself in the kitchen, Hudson, Sebastian and Harry right behind me. I glared at Sebastian. "Leave us." Harry zipped out of the room.

Sebastian frowned. "Something has happened."

"This will only take a few minutes. Given my specialty is the dead, I'm sure a few minutes won't matter."

Sebastian narrowed his gaze on Hudson. "You hurt her and the pack will be finding themselves a new Principal." Then the crown Prince of America stormed out of the kitchen, the door swinging closed behind him.

I narrowed my eyes on Hudson. "I want you to stop pursuing me."

He folded his arms. "No."

I threw my arms up. "Why? You could have any woman you want. Why bother with little old me? A mediocre witch with ex-boyfriend issues? I would bore you before the end of the night. We have nothing in common, and our very species puts us at odds. Which means for you it would be a roll in the sack before you return to your shifter honeys."

"You have this all figured out."

I leaned back against the sink. "I do."

"So you want me to leave you alone because you think I want a one-night stand?"

No, I want you to leave me alone because I think I would struggle to put myself back together when you left me. "That's right."

His nostrils flared, and he took a step towards me. Then another. His hands caged me against the sink. I tipped my head back and looked up at him. "You want extraordinary?"

"I do."

"What if that is what I give you?"

I blinked. "In a world where I become your mate, I would be forced to move home, leave my job, family and friends. I would risk you draining me of my magic."

"I don't need your magic."

"And I don't need you."

"Which is part of what attracts me to you. Do you know how many females hang on my tail, wanting the big bad Terror of Tennessee to protect them? Then when reality slaps them in the face that I can't be tamed, they run and hide. It's a huge turnoff."

"You're a freaking sabre-tooth tiger, Hudson. Females who think that you can be tamed don't make it into double digits on the IQ scale."

His thumbs brushed against my ribs. "So you know, and yet still go toe to toe with me."

"You don't scare me."

"I should."

"Ever thought it's you who should fear me?"

He blinked, his thumbs stilling on my sides. Then he threw his head back and laughed. He pulled back with a bright smile. "Okay, little witch, you win this round."

My stomach plummeted. Why? Because he'd conceded and was now going to leave me alone. At least my mouth was being smart. "So you'll leave me alone?"

His hand came towards my face, his thumb brushed against my bottom lip. My lips parted and my breath hitched. His gaze focused on my mouth. "No, I will work on being extraordinary."

CHAPTER SEVENTEEN

Tick, tick, tick... boom.

I grabbed orange juice and cookies. The staple diet of someone that burns through sugar when working. My aunts would have already left or Aunt Liz would already be up preparing breakfast and Aunt Dayna would be meditating in the middle of the parlor floor. I find Hudson and Sebastian mumbling to each other in the parlor. They spin to look at me as I enter. "So who's dead?"

Sebastian frowned and shoved his hands in his pockets. "William Wilson, head of house Wilson."

I squeezed his arm. "I'm sorry."

"Jennifer McAllister is also dead, a wolf shifter in the pack," Hudson added. "This is why I came to get you. Dave tried calling, he thinks you should see her in situ, maybe you can see something we are missing."

"I'm not a trained criminal investigator," I pointed out.

Hudson gave me a tight smile. "I know, you are better."

I blinked. "Okay, I need to grab a few things before we go to see William, then Jennifer."

Hudson's growl rumbled from his throat. Sebastian cocked an eyebrow at him. "It's fine," Sebastian said, "I need to smooth things over with the Wilson family before you come. Call me when you are done."

Sebastian wrapped me in a quick hug. "You smell of him," he muttered in my ear.

I smacked the back of his head. "Go, I will be along to visit your vampire soon."

He zoomed out of the house; the door clicking shut a few seconds later. "Let me grab my bag, then we can get going."

I hurried down the stairs, into my lab and grabbed a few tools I might need, evidence bags, and a couple of bottles of the magenta liquid Aunt Anita had cooked up before she left. I dragged my wild hair up into a bun and plucked my grey linen jacket from the back of my office chair.

Hudson was waiting by the garage door, a frown settled on his face. Oh boy. Here we go. I snatched the Bugatti keys from the hook next to the door and entered the garage. Five, four, three…

"Are you sure this is a good idea?" he said as I dropped into the driver's seat. He folded himself into the passenger side and I clipped my seat belt on before peeling out of the garage.

"It was your idea," I pointed out, indicating left onto the main road out of White Castle. He let out a tremendous sigh.

"The last time you examined a body, it blew up and brought a building down. Had I not been there…"

I let the words hang between us; I was stronger than he gave me credit for. I might have been injured, but I wouldn't have died. The best course of action here was to play to his alpha bullshit. "Well you were there, and you'll be here again. You know, so you can save the damsel in distress."

"You're no damsel."

A smile stretched my lips. "I know. Where was Jennifer found?"

"The pack house," he gritted out. I shot him a quick look before refocusing on the road. The killer had come into the most secure location in the pack and murdered one of their own. He was beating himself up for not being there.

"It wouldn't have made a difference," I said.

"You don't know that."

"Not yet," I conceded. "But he wanted your attention and now he's got it."

Silence loomed between us for several minutes as I zoomed towards the pack house. "It's not my attention he wants," Hudson finally said.

I frowned. "What do you mean?"

"It's yours."

"Then why not leave a body on my doorstep?"

"He tried that. We brought the bodies to you. No, he wants something from you. What could that be?"

I took a deep breath. "He might misunderstand my gift."

"Explain."

"Retros are so rare, many people haven't even heard of them. Precogs, whilst scarce, are more coveted and sometimes hunted for their abilities."

"Why kill people then? That speaks of a man who knows exactly what you are."

No one but me, my maker, and my parents knew exactly what I was. My mother was dead, my father was MIA, and I am fairly confident none of them were hunting vampires and shifters to get to me. "Okay, so if we assume he's trying to get to me. He now knows who I am. Why keep killing? Why not just come at me head on?"

"He tried that, twice. If I knew what he wanted with you, I might have more of a chance at unravelling this."

"When you figure it out, let me know."

I pulled through a set of gates and drove up the steep drive towards a sprawling Scandinavian-style wooden lodge, with floor to ceiling windows lit up like a Christmas tree. Seating scattered the wrap-around porch. Each corner had balconies jutting out on the first floor, with iron railings and steps leading to the ground. A hint of the lowest level peeked up from below the hill, hiding behind stones. "At some point you can also let me know how you know where the pack house is."

Shit. Shit, shit, shit. I almost banged my head on the steering wheel. The pack house location wasn't a widely advertised fact. I opened my mouth. "Don't lie to me," Hudson growled. "If you aren't going to tell me the truth, then refrain from speaking." I snapped my mouth closed.

Wow, he was mega pissed. I stopped the car and killed the engine. I swiveled in my seat to face him. "There are things I can't tell you."

He rolled his eyes. "Are we back to making you sound more interesting than you actually are?"

I blinked. "We are certainly back to you being an asshole." I grabbed my bag, popped the door open and climbed out.

"Cora," Hudson said. I slammed the door and jogged up the steps, ignoring his majesty. Dave opened the door. A frown appeared between his brows as he looked over my shoulder. "Cora," Hudson tried again.

"Are you going to let me in?" I asked Dave.

"What happened with you two?"

"He can't handle not knowing every facet of my life. If I don't want to tell him something, I am a liar, or trying to make myself more interesting. There's just one issue in his theory."

"And what's that?" Hudson said from right behind me.

"I don't want to seem more interesting to you. In fact, if you never spoke to me again, that would be perfect."

"When this is over, consider your wish granted."

My heart gave a tiny twang. It's what I wanted, right? "I'll work on being extraordinary, Cora," I muttered to myself. "Glad to know you were committed to that statement."

Dave looked between us, shook his head and spun on his heel. "Follow me."

He led us through the sitting room with scattered neutral colored sofas and cushions. Wooden beams sprouted across the ceiling, the matching floor making the house warm and inviting. It was built for a large family.

"How many people live here?" I asked.

Dave glanced at me over his shoulder as he pushed through a door. "Officially one." He looked over my head to Hudson. "But I often stay, and some enforcers."

We entered the kitchen; it was a large affair with pans hanging from the rafters. A long island sat in the middle of the tiled floor. On it lay the body of a curvy woman dressed in jeans and a plain white T-shirt. Her blonde hair was splayed out around her and her blue eyes were trained on us as if she was viewing us from beyond the grave. A wave of sadness made my muscles sag. Such a pointless waste of a life. For what? To get my attention? It was looking more and more like I would have to take the plunge and call the Order. No one wanted the scrutiny of the Order upon them. No one wanted to be examined by the tyrannical bitch that was quick to judge and even quicker to punish.

"No visible wounds, no signs of a struggle, just like the others," Dave muttered.

My bag sank onto the kitchen table and I dug around for the magenta potion bottle. Dave eyeballed the liquid. "What's that?"

"A neutralizer."

I snapped on some gloves and stepped up to Jennifer. She was so pretty, had so much to live for, a bright future cut short by a man on a mission nobody freaking understood. I tipped the liquid into my palms and rubbed it into my gloves. Then I grasped her hand and pushed the spell into her body. A wall of resistance met my power, I prodded it until it popped then the magic travelled around her body neutralizing the bomb he had planted inside her.

"Was there a bomb?" Dave asked.

I nodded, stepped back and pulled my gloves off. "Yes."
I glanced around the kitchen. "Bin?" Dave pointed towards
the double patio doors. I strode forward and dropped my
gloves in the bin. "Was the door open?" I asked as I peered
into the night.

"Yes," Hudson said. "It's always open." Figures. Who
would come to tackle the Principal of North America? A
psychotic elemental with a death wish.

I stood next to Jennifer and turned to Dave and Hudson.
"You need to leave," I stated.

Hudson shook his head. "You are vulnerable when you
do this. You need someone here."

Dave nodded. "Even if it's someone to catch you if you
fall. There's only so many times you can bump that brain of
yours and not get a concussion."

Hudson sighed. "Even if we sat on the other side of the
house. We could be here in seconds. There are no locks to
keep us out."

I flattened my lips. They were right. In my blind
agreement to come and figure this out, I'd walked myself
into a vulnerable position.

"What do you think we are going to do?" Hudson asked. He flipped on his alpha stare, I knew I should back down but that would make me prey. Green rolled over his eyes as his beast peered out at me. His nostrils flared. He folded his arms.

"Fine," I conceded. "But you must not interfere, no matter what I say, do, or look like. You must not speak to me or wake me up."

Hudson's eyes narrowed. "Why? What happens?"

I spun towards Jennifer and steadied myself for what was to come. "I relive their death, and whilst most deaths are a peaceful affair, these are full of agony. He wants me to suffer, so they do. If you wake me up mid read, I might get stuck in that memory."

"For how long?" Hudson asked.

"Eternity," I muttered and grasped Jennifer's hand before I could change my mind about the two males in the room. The vision sucked me down, I was outside the pack house coming up the wooden steps to the porch. "Hudson," I called out. My voice had a sultry timber. I pushed open the front door. "Hudson, where are you?" I said with excitement. Jennifer and Hudson were intimate, and she was here seeking him out whilst he was rolling around with me on my bedroom floor. I prowled through the sitting room, my fingers brushing against the cushions as I went. Something clanged in the kitchen. A smile crept across my face as I made my way towards it. I pushed open the door and froze. A cloaked figure turned from the window and faced me. His eyes promised pain. He snapped his fingers. Numbness travelled down my left side, like liquid ice. My sluggish hand moved to my throat as my wolf tried to growl a warning at the intruder. He smelled strange. I leaned against the island.

"Let's get you up there shall we?" Ric stated, scooping his arm under my legs, the other banded around my back. My legs gave way just as he swept me up and laid me down on the kitchen island. I tried to move my mouth to scream, but it was like someone had cut my vocal chords. Tears formed in my eyes. He placed his index finger over my lips. "Shush, you are having a major stroke. You won't be able to move or scream whilst I deliver my message to Cora." He leaned over me and smiled. "Cora Roberts, when you wake from this you'll see I've delivered you some instructions. I'd say come alone, but we all know the beast will follow you, the bloodsucker too. So you and them only." His finger trailed from my lips down my throat. Panic flared through me. He was going to do something sexual. His finger hooked under my T-shirt and dragged it up, exposing my abdomen. He smirked. "This is going to hurt like a bitch."

Blazing hot fire broke out across my stomach. Inside I was screaming so loud heaven and hell would hear. Outside, I couldn't move. He took his time torturing my flesh before stepping back and tilting his head. He pulled the T-shirt down. Then an orb of pale pink magic appeared in his left palm. He winked at me. "This little present is also going to hurt." He grasped my chin and pried it open before stuffing the magic down my throat. He massaged it so I would swallow. No, no, no… I needed out of this memory now. But I was trapped inside Jennifer's body and Jennifer couldn't move, talk, or scream. Tears streamed down the sides of my face, the incredible pressure of the magic making my chest ache. He placed his hand over my mouth and pinched my nose.

"Time to die," he muttered, a sick look of pleasure in his eyes as he watched my life slip away. I fought against the feeling. It's not real, it's not real, I chanted to myself. I felt

Jennifer's acceptance of her fate and clawed my subconscious from hers. He snapped the fingers of his other hand and magic exploded in my chest. Another bomb… one I hadn't disabled. The present came back blurry. My face was wet with tears and my chest held an ache I understood too well. My body slumped, I got halfway to the floor before muscular arms wrapped around me from behind.

"I got you," Hudson said in my ear.

I held onto the kitchen island with white knuckles. Dave handed me a tissue. I dabbed my eyes, bringing the room back into focus. Dave's face was tight with worry. "That's what you go through every time?"

I shook my head and leaned back against Hudson, I just needed a minute before I looked. "I go through whatever they went through."

Hudson's arms tightened around me. "But you were screaming like the world was on fire."

"She had a stroke, she was paralyzed while he tortured her, she couldn't scream for help, but believe me she was trying."

I tapped Hudson's forearm. He held me another few seconds, then dropped them with a sigh. "Can you pass me a set of gloves out of my bag?" I asked Hudson.

He dropped them in my outstretched hand whilst I leaned against the island. I pulled them on, then reached forward to Jennifer's T-shirt. Dave's hand snapped out and caught my wrist. "What are you doing?"

I was trembling from low sugar and the magic Ric had set off. "I'm fairly certain the killer has left us a message."

Dave glanced over my shoulder at Hudson and released my wrist. I dragged the T-shirt up, revealing a long series of two numbers etched into her skin. "What in the fresh hell is this?" Hudson growled, moving beside me.

"Co-ordinates," I slurred. Ah shit, this was going to suck donkey balls. Dave's head snapped up. He studied me.

"What's wrong?" he asked.

"Find out where this is for when I wake up," I garbled out.

Hudson spun me towards him and I slumped forward into his chest. Great, I was throwing myself at the Terror of Tennessee. He wouldn't let me live this down.

"Get Norbert," Hudson shouted.

"No doctor can help me," I mumbled against his T-shirt. He smelt nice, like the forest on a dewy morning. "I just need sleep."

"You're a fucking mess, you'll be seen by a doctor."

"I am a doctor."

He swung me up in his arms, bridal style. "Humor me."

"It didn't work."

"What didn't?"

"Don't pretend you didn't bring me out here to see if you can lure out the killer on your own turf. I'm bait."

We started up some stairs. His face tightened as the shadows of my mind claimed me. "It didn't work."

I huffed out a laugh seconds before I went to pass out. "It got me out and away from my home and even if it didn't it's left me without..." A jolt of terror whipped through me. "Hudson, the house, Rebecca, Maggie... I left them vulnerable."

CHAPTER EIGHTEEN

Torture affects you on a soul deep level. The scars are just

for show.

I opened my eyes to find a fan whirling above me. Sunlight streamed through the windows and bathed the four-poster monster of a bed I was lying on in warmth. My hands dragged across the sheets, ugh soft, soft, sheets that felt like I was lying on a cloud. I closed my eyes. I could just rest another hour or two, maybe. Wherever I was, people couldn't find me to demand my attention. I didn't need to deal with any disputes in the house, nobody was calling me to psychically dissect the deceased's last moments.

Someone cleared their throat to my left. It was a deep sound. I rubbed my hand over my face. The second I reopened my eyes, I would need to deal with... my eyes snapped open and I jerked upright.

I looked to my left. Hudson sat in an armchair, elbows on his knees, leaning towards me, a deep frown on his face. The door behind him opened and Dave stepped through, a grim look that spelled bad news on his face. The sun was well past its highest point. That wasn't good.

"The bloodsucker will be here in a few minutes, I couldn't keep him away any longer," Dave said to Hudson. "The house has been cleared, hopefully there won't be any run-ins."

I blinked. "Sebastian is coming here?"

"I've updated him on everything."

Hudson didn't take his eyes off me. "Do you remember mumbling about the house and your family being left vulnerable?"

I nodded and dug around in my psyche, finding what I expected. "We went to check on them," Dave said, running his hand through his hair. "The entire household was knocked out cold." I held my breath. That wasn't the end.

Hudson grabbed something from the bedside table and threw it on my lap. I slapped my hand over my mouth. A Polaroid picture of Maggie, bound at the wrists and ankles with thick rope, stared back at me. Her hair was matted with blood, her right eye swollen shut, and her lips were split. She'd put up a fight. "This was attached to the front door," Hudson said. He flipped the picture over, 10pm written on the other side.

"Why does he want you?" Hudson said, so quiet I had to strain to hear him.

I shook my head. "I don't know."

Hudson shot to his feet, the armchair flipping onto its back behind him. His arms came down beside mine and he got in my face. I didn't move. "What aren't you telling me?"

"Nothing."

His roar had me shrinking back, but I held the alpha stare he was leveling my way. He terrified me, but backing down would make for a lifetime of trouble. His hand wrapped around my throat. "This killer purposefully targets shifters and vampires until he finally gets a lock on you, the only known retro in America. Then he attacks your house and your family and leaves you little love notes—but you don't know what he wants?"

My brows tightened. He'd put all that together. "You said it yourself, I'm the only known retro—he obviously wants me for that reason."

"What could he want with a girl who can see the last moments of someone's life?"

"He's psychotic. I'm sure his reasons make sense to him alone."

Hudson leaned in closer. "Is he an elemental?"

"Yes," I whispered. His eyes widened, and he backed up, picked up the chair and sat himself back down. Dave remained frozen at the end of the bed.

"You want me to call the Order?" I asked.

Dave snorted a laugh as Hudson rolled his eyes. "The Order will turn a fight into a war. This is one rogue elemental demanding the attention of another. He's prodding at the other factions for a reaction. Most fanatics need attention. The more we give him, the more fanfare he will provide in the way of bodies and death. We need to keep this low key. Right now me, you and Dave know he's an elemental. Unless we can't put an end to this tonight, let's just keep this to ourselves."

"Okay," I mumbled. So the large dumb beast was actually more of a political badass than I gave him credit for. Go figure.

"So your life for Maggie's," Hudson said, picking up the photograph as if I hadn't just admitted my faction murdered his.

I closed my eyes and pictured her alone and scared. "I need your help."

Dave scoffed. "She's not pack; we aren't obligated to provide any protection or charge in on any rescue mission."

That slimy, conniving... "I'm calling in my favor."

Dave's fists tightened. "Damn it."

Hudson sighed. "You want us to help rescue Maggie?"

I nodded. "Yes, and no. I want you to treat her as if she was pack, and when we rescue her, give her the option of joining the pack."

Dave groaned. "We can't just permit anyone..."

"Done," Hudson overruled him. He reached out for my arm, I reciprocated, and we grasped forearms in the tradition of pack members making a promise which if broken, you could demand the life of the breaker. Pack promises were not to be scoffed at.

"Why?" he asked.

"Why what?"

"Why risk your life for a shifter?"

I sighed as an image of the thin and vulnerable Maggie begging for a home to be safe in, presented itself in my mind. "She's one of mine. When nobody else would protect her, I took her in. She's my responsibility." This is why the packs politics leaves something to be desired. "She ran because she was being forced at 18 into an arranged marriage. The things she'd already endured by the hands of that male and his friends should be illegal."

"I outlawed arranged marriages years ago. Why didn't she tell her alpha?"

I threw my head back and laughed. It was brittle. "Maggie is the alpha's daughter."

He sighed. "There are four thousand three hundred and sixty-one packs under my care." Yes, yes, you have lots of subjects. "Changing the ways of any people takes time. Not everyone agrees with my laws, and there are those that break the law. She could have come to me."

"She was 17, traumatized, homeless and terrified. They had made her believe everything that was happening was legal, and it was her duty as the alpha's daughter to marry whom her parents chose without question. When she arrived on my doorstep, she was a hair's breadth away from a total breakdown and the pack was the last place she felt safe. She believed you condoned the mating."

"Believed?"

I sighed and played with the end of the sheets. "It took months, but I explained the pack laws, *your* laws. Some careful visits from local loner families in the area drew her out of her shell. The Maggie you know now is a beautiful, confident young woman finding her way in the world, but she misses her pack. I can never replace that sense of family she has lost. Maybe with you she can."

"You are both missing the important thing," Dave said. "We have to get her back alive before she can decide her future residence."

"Did you find the location?" I asked.

Hudson nodded. "It's an abandoned farm, I've had two scouts out there already. He's in there. He left his stench around the boundary and some powerful wards."

I picked up the photo of Maggie and twisted it around in my hand. "He said I could bring you."

Hudson folded his arms. "When?"

"In the retro read. He said I could bring the beast."

"Good, with your magic and my strength we should be able to nail him."

I shook my head, dropped the picture and looked up to meet Hudson's stare. "I don't have any magic."

He blinked. "Cora, you demonstrated clearly a few nights ago you have more magic than anyone realized."

"There was a bomb, a psychic one. When I read Jennifer, it exploded and neutralized my magic."

Silence coated the room as we scrambled for a plan that wouldn't end in me being dissected by Ric. There wasn't one. But I wouldn't let Maggie die because I was too chicken to face my foe. The door burst open and Sebastian stepped through. His eyes swept the room before landing on my pathetic ass.

"Psychic bomb?" he asked. I nodded. "You sure?"

My eyes tightened and my heart bounced around in my chest. "I'm sure."

"It's like last time?"

"Last time?" Dave and Hudson parroted.

I glared at Sebastian. "Stronger. I might recover my magic in the next week or two."

He scrubbed a hand down his face, ignoring the audience we had, and settled onto the bed beside me. He tucked an arm around my shoulders. "So you don't go, we go instead."

I tipped my head up to look at him. "Not happening. If he doesn't see me first, he will kill Maggie."

His scowl deepened. "Do you know what he wants with you?" I bit my lip and shook my head.

Hudson smacked his hand down on the bed. The bed shifted to the right a few inches with the force. "What aren't you telling me?"

"I'm not telling you many things."

"She's withholding that someone once kidnapped and tortured her because of her gift," Sebastian ground out.

"Shut up," I snapped.

"An elemental?" Hudson said with a frown as he tried to piece this part of my life together.

Sebastian shook his head. "No, by her shifter boyfriend and his friends."

"Sebastian!" My stomach twisted and I looked around, calculating my chances of escape from this room before he could go any further.

"I can't hold your broken body again and wonder if I am going to be enough to fix you this time. Once was enough, then again this week. Now you're asking me to let you just wander into the arms of a monster who will do god knows what to you."

"I'm asking you to not air my dirty laundry out in front of strangers."

"If that keeps your ass out of danger, then so be it."

"How?" Hudson growled low, it rumbled through the room.

I blinked at him, then at Dave. "How what?"

"How did he torture you?"

I ran my hands through my hair, tugging on the strands. "Fine, you want a show and tell?" I yanked the sheets down and lifted my T-shirt up. The small wounds from the explosion this week had healed. But the stripes of scars, white and faded, shone in the sunlight. Hudson looked over them, his face blanked. I twisted up onto my knees and showed him my back. Nobody moved.

The words left my mouth in a monotone ramble as I disassociated myself from the memory. "They whipped me with a belt, buckle side, imbued with a potion to make sure it didn't heal. When that didn't get them what they wanted, I was waterboarded, poorly... they almost lost me three times. That's when they dislocated various joints, removed nails, electrocuted me even. Cattle prods, tasers... whatever was at hand. Someone had supplied him with a magic nulling potion, so I couldn't fight back."

I dropped my T-shirt and spun, expecting to see pity splashed across Hudson's face. It wasn't; I was met with the blank face of the Principal. He studied my face for a long stretch of time. His jaw ticked as he ground his teeth. "Why?" he finally asked.

"Why? Because I trusted the wrong person with my secrets. My boyfriend heard visions and assumed Precog. He and his friends starved and tortured me for over a week. They wanted to know the next lottery numbers, or which stocks to invest in. They wanted me to make them rich. The more I explained, the harder the beatings got." Sebastian put his hand on my shoulder. I shrugged him off. "On day eight, Sebastian came looking for me, to argue over the fact I'd scored higher than him in the finals. He followed the scent of blood and death until he found me."

"I'd never seen anyone in so much pain skirting the edge of death like she was," Sebastian added. "I will never forget the look of utter fear in her eyes as I entered the room. I only wished I'd had more time to spend on their deaths. They got off too easy."

Hudson closed his eyes and breathed in. "You never reported it," he said. "Why?"

"They were dead, what more was there to do?"

"This is when you first shared your blood with her?" Hudson asked Sebastian.

"Yes."

"Did they do anything else?" Dave asked.

My head snapped to his. "Is that not enough?"

Dave leveled me with a hard stare. "Did they—"

"Stop," I whispered. The emotional pain was a hundredfold more powerful than the physical. I hid deep the worst of my scars within. Neil had twisted my personality with his betrayal. I could never trust someone like that again. I had too much to hide, and so much to lose. "You know enough. Those were the most horrific days of my life. This brief trip down memory lane needs to stop. You've pried deep into my psyche; my demons have been splayed out for you to see. Now let's focus on getting Maggie back."

"I'm coming," Sebastian stated.

I rolled my eyes. "Yeah, you me and beast. That's his demand."

Dave frowned. "If he wanted to trigger a war between factions, attacking the Principal and crown prince of America would be a sure-fire way to do it."

"He's happy for you to come along because to him, an elemental with powerful magic, you pose no threat. I'm powerless, so I'm easy game."

"Is there any way of getting your magic back sooner?" Dave asked.

I shook my head. "No, I'll have to wait it out. But… what if we could even the playing field?" I slid from the bed and paced the room as the cogs in my brain churned over ideas.

"I have a plan," I announced.

Hudson's eyebrow hooked up as he looked me over. I glanced at myself in the mirror. My hair was stuck out at odd angles, and I was still in yesterday's jeans and T-shirt. Even the Queen of England sleeps in something comfy - doesn't mean she can't plot stuff at the same time.

"It requires sacrifice, pain and effort," I added.

Dave folded his arms across his chest. "I hate it already."

"We'll need to be stealthy."

Hudson laughed. "With you? We're doomed."

I planted my hands on my hips. "I'm stealthy, like a B-2 bomber."

He smirked at me. "Whilst I'm mildly turned on that you can spout random aircraft facts, you're as stealthy as a baby elephant parading for the first time in the street."

"We can't all creep around like phantoms."

He grinned, all teeth on show. "Not phantoms, cats."

Oh boy.

CHAPTER NINETEEN

I'll show you mine if you show me yours.

Sebastian, Hudson and I left the pack house bundled into an SUV. I was trying to ignore the fact that the ghost of Jennifer was sitting next to Sebastian in the back seat. She'd spent the first few minutes trying to put her seatbelt on.

"Did you know Jennifer well?" I asked. Hudson side-eyed me as he accelerated. A nanosecond later, I regretted asking. I sounded like a jealous girlfriend.

"Yes."

"Were you two together?" Come on, brain, knock it off. You told him no, remember? Twice. Sebastian chuckled.

Jennifer ignored the entire conversation, more invested in breaching the divide between life and death to click her seatbelt in place. Safety first I guess.

Hudson's lips tilted up. "Jennifer was a beautiful wolf with a kind temperament." I huffed. "But, we grew up together in the pack. She was more like a little sister. I would terrify her like most of my kind. It's a turn-off to have someone shrink in terror every time you remotely lose your shit. No, my mate needs to stand up to alpha bullshit and pull me up when I cross a line." He glanced at me again. "Left with a weaker mate, my beast would be unhappy."

I blinked. I think the Terror of Tennessee just complimented me. Summer Grove House came into view as Hudson swung the pack's SUV through the gates.

"I don't know how you can eat that stuff," Sebastian said, breaking the tension. I looked over my shoulder at him and stuffed the last piece of beef jerky in my mouth from the family sized tub. It was the only decent junk food I could scavenge from Hudson's kitchen.

"I need to eat or I'll crash again," I mumbled. "And we have less than three hours to get the stuff we need and get our asses to the farm."

"You have visitors," Hudson said. I spun to the front and found the sheriff's car parked at the bottom of the steps. The man in question was standing outside my front door, his hands on his hips, looking utterly lost.

"Wonderful, the local law enforcement is here to help, we're all saved," I muttered with a sigh as I opened the door and jumped out of the car.

I plastered a smile as bright as the Louisiana sun on my face and began walking towards Robert. He skimmed the gun at his waist with his hand. He was in jeans and a shirt. Another unofficial visit. "How can I help you, Sheriff?" I asked, jogging up the steps toward the door.

Robert ignored me in favor of analyzing Hudson and Sebastian. So he was here for them and didn't know how to find them, so he'd hung out by my doorstep until they showed.

"I have questions," Robert began.

Sebastian gave him a tight smile, Hudson stormed past him without a glance. "Not now," he growled, opening the door and entering my home. I followed Sebastian with Robert behind me.

"We're a little busy," I explained, waving the empty beef jerky tub in my hand like it had all the answers. "Supernatural shenanigans and whatnot."

Robert closed the door and folded his arms. I sighed at his hard look. In his head, what could be more important than describing an entire hidden world to him? Rebecca came barreling down the stairs, eyes wide and hair disheveled. She ran right into me and wrapped me in a hug. Harry floated behind her. "Miss Roberts! Thank the lord you are well. Miss. Lexington has taken young Maggie's kidnapping hard." He scanned Sebastian and Hudson. "I see you have brought your male suitors to help with the rescue mission."

"Not good enough, Cora, I need answers now," Robert said. I was too tired to hold conversations with the dead and living at the same time. "No one leaves until I understand exactly what's happening here."

Someone pounded on the door. I blinked. Without my magic, my wards weren't functioning, which meant no supernatural warning system. Robert spun and opened the door. Jennifer drifted in first, eyes wide as saucers as she took in my home. My brain faltered. Did ghosts knock now?

How polite. Then Matthew Walker, a butch balding man with sleeve tattoos came blasting through the door shaking his fist. "Dr Roberts, you guaranteed these tablets would cure my problem!"

I raised a brow and swept my hands towards the staircase leading toward my office. I had zero time to deal with irate shifters. "Would you like to follow me downstairs?"

Matthew was blind to the mismatched audience who stood with equal parts astonishment, amusement and accusation. He dug his hand into his inside coat pocket. Hudson moved as if to stop him. I rolled my eyes. Matthew glared at me and rattled a large pill bottle at me. "No, Dr. Roberts, I want you to explain why you've sold me stuff that does nothing but give me an upset stomach."

Okay, he asked for it. I dropped my voice as if that would save him from the overachieving hearing of the supes. "That's because they don't go in your mouth, Matthew."

"Then where the hell are they meant to go?"

I quirked a brow and glanced down. "Oh, oh!" He glanced round at the room. The sheriff, a princess, a prince, and the Principal of his own species wore amused looks at his expense. Matthew rubbed the back of his head. "My bad, Dr. Roberts, next time I'll read the instructions."

Men - they refused to read instructions. The man heard one at night and just swallowed it down. Idiot.

He shuffled towards the door, swinging a sheepish glance at Hudson. He opened the door and a ball of furious white fur shot between his legs. She halted in front of Robert. The door clicked shut as Matthew left.

"What did you treat him for?" Rebecca asked.

I shook my head. "Patient confidentiality."

"Erectile dysfunction," Sebastian announced. I massaged my temples as he shrugged. "What? He wasn't my patient."

Bella dropped a mouse at the foot of the sheriff and gave me the side-eye. I glared at her. She swished her tail and narrowed her eyes. "You have got to be kidding me," I mumbled. The sheriff reached down and patted her on her head.

"Pretty cat," Robert said. She licked his hand. What a floozy.

"Who are you?" Harry asks Jennifer.

Jennifer blinks at him and looks behind her. She points to herself. "Me?" I rubbed my temples.

Oh boy. Hudson turns to the Sheriff. "One of my own has been kidnapped by the psychopathic monster that you met on Cora's doorstep a few nights ago. He's clear on his deadline. I don't have time to answer all your inane human questions right now."

Wow, way to endear the human to us. Robert's arms dropped to his sides. "What can I do?"

"Stay here, guard the house," I stated.

Harry puffed up his chest. "That's my job."

"You I need," I said.

Everyone looked at each other in confusion. "Who?" Sebastian said. Save me now.

Jennifer pointed at her chest. "Me?"

I shook my head. "Sorry, I'm just trying to work through the plan in my head and I'm tired."

"Not you, the role of ghost sidekick has been taken," Harry declared. Jennifer shouldn't be here. She was on consecrated ground. Then again, Harry shouldn't be here either. I couldn't lead Jennifer into the other room in my apartments right now because it would knock me out for hours.

"Sebastian, could you show the Sheriff around the house, make sure he knows where every entrance is." I turned to Hudson. "If Rebecca gets you the runes, could you place them around the perimeter of the property, my wards are down."

He nodded. My gaze darted between Harry and Jennifer. "I will be at least an hour, but I'll meet you back in the parlor when I have everything I need. And can someone get rid of that mouse?" The journey up the stairs was hard. My muscles ached, fatigue plagued my mind, and I considered whether the hour I had would be better spent asleep. If my aunts were still here, they could make the potion, as it was they had left for their respective homes across the country.

Harry floated next to me. "Miss Roberts, what are we going to do with the female interloper?"

I sighed and pushed through my apartment door. Jennifer hovered in the hallway. "Jennifer, come inside."

She whipped her head up and flew straight at me, opening her arms. I gritted my teeth. She passed straight through me. A shiver danced from my nape to the base of my spine. I shut the door and spun to my ghosts. "Harry, this is Jennifer. Harry is a recently murdered vampire,

Jennifer is a recently murdered shifter. The same man murdered you both, you have that in common."

They eyed each other. "I don't know why I'm here," Jennifer said.

I shook my head. "Me either, your body would have already been taken to shifter consecrated ground. There is zero reason for you to still be wandering the Earth." I walked to the kitchen and opened the floor-to-ceiling cabinet. I grabbed the dried rosemary, lavender and mint and placed them on the chopping board. I selected bottles of powdered ginger, turmeric and cloves.

"What are you doing?" Harry asked. "Aren't you going to help Jennifer?" He waved at the locked door. Jennifer looked at it.

"Not now, I need to make this potion, eat and hydrate. Then I need to take down your murderer. If I help Jennifer, it will knock me out for hours. I'm already running on fumes."

"Help me how?" Jennifer asked.

I found my pestle and mortar and began grinding the plants and herbs. "I'll explain when I get back. In the meantime, I need your help. You up for a little reconnaissance work?" Harry stood to attention. Jennifer drifted next to him. *Cora Roberts, general of a ghost army*.

Meadow Farm was an oxymoron. It was a collection of dilapidated buildings surrounded by diminished grass and dust. Hudson, Sebastian and I sat on the outskirts of the property; about a quarter of a mile from what I assumed was once the dwelling. Half of the roof was missing, and the windows were boarded up or smashed. The sun was quickly retreating to its grave behind the farm, and soon I would be without sight. The air was still, poised for the battle that was likely coming. I scanned the area and waited for Harry and Jennifer.

"How long now?" Hudson growled out.

"Be patient, this takes time," I replied. Come on, guys. A flash of blonde hair had my eyes narrowing in on a figure moving towards me at speed.

"I don't understand how you are going to identify where Maggie is without your magic."

"Just because I'm without magic doesn't make me powerless," I mumbled as Jennifer came to a stop in front of me.

"Maggie is alive and being held in the farmhouse, top floor, master bedroom at the end of the hall," Jennifer jabbered. I gave her a subtle nod.

"Okay, Maggie is in the farmhouse, last bedroom on the top floor."

Hudson frowned, Sebastian nodded. He didn't know this secret, but our friendship meant he trusted me. "And the killer?" Hudson asked.

I looked at Jennifer. She shook her head. "Harry is still searching for him."

"I can't sense him," I said.

"For this plan to work, you need to find him," Hudson stated.

"I'm aware."

Sebastian checked his watch. "It's time," he stated. We stalked forward, our steps eating up the dusty road as we headed toward a situation I couldn't control and could barely defend against. We just had to get Maggie out.

Jennifer hovered in front of me, staring at the ground, drifting backwards. "There's something holding Maggie down. A creature, not a shifter and not a vampire. I've never seen anything like it." Her head shot up and her pretty eyes bored into mine. "It's evil given form."

Of course it was. I swallowed down my fear. Sebastian shot me a curious look. "We don't know what we are facing, so we stick to the plan. Getting Maggie out is our priority," I stated.

"Agreed," Sebastian said. I side eyed Hudson, who gave a sharp nod. His eyes rolled green as he studied the property.

I took a steadying breath and stuffed my hand in my coat pocket, massaging the orb to remind myself it was still there.

We halted in the clearing. "Ric Nichols, I am here as requested, release my friend," I called out. Nothing moved. I nudged Sebastian's arm. "Go find Maggie."

He shot into the farm building. Hudson stalked amongst the ramshackle buildings, leaving me alone and prone, just like we planned. The fabric of the universe spilt thirty yards in front of me and Ric stepped out, his eyes blacker than the night sky. He smiled, showing me sharp teeth. Was it cosmetic or a spell that he'd done to get those spiky beauties? The jagged tear sealed behind him. I couldn't fathom how he'd done that. Elementals didn't mess with the universe, because the universe had a way of messing back. "So you can follow instructions. That should make this easier," he drawled, taking a step closer. That's right, keep coming, asshole.

"Make what easier?" I asked. Please let him be a typical book villain that tells us his nefarious intentions at length, giving time for the hero to save the day. Something large prowled between the buildings. I worked to keep my attention on Ric.

Ric started circling me, I rotated with him an inch at a time. "You will open a portal for myself and my brethren to escape through. It's time for us to rise, but Earth isn't our destination. We want the very top."

I frowned. His brethren? Portals? Ric was nuts. "I don't understand."

He sighed. "I know what you do with the dead, I want you to open that gateway for me to follow."

"You want into my world? Why?"

He shook his head. "Not your world."

"But that is what I do, I have built a world for the lonely dead to find peace."

He threw his head back and laughed. "You are so naïve. You haven't built an afterlife for them, you've given them a direct line to the afterlife only meant for the good."

"Wait. What?"

"The portal you open, bypassing the gates of heaven, allows any creature entrance to the promised land. You are literally playing God." I blinked and the gut feeling of this truth hit me like a freight train. Ric tutted. "Did you know the shifter in the trailer park was a child sex offender from out of county? He dreamt of tiny little girls and only regretted that they had ever caught him. It marked his soul for the depths of hell, but you swanned in and played judge and jury, and sent him to live his afterlife in peace and light when it should be in pain and darkness."

I shook my head and took a step back. "No," I whispered.

"You will open a portal so I can enter heaven with my army and take it for myself."

"What army?"

306

A horrific scream shattered the silence. The pain vibrated into my soul. Maggie. A creature as tall as the house stepped out of the shadows, it's straggly limbs making it lurch as it came towards us. An identical creature rose from the ground near the farm buildings. Then another. They had no defining facial features. They were surrounding us. Forming a wall of horror from which I would never escape.

"Do you know what you are?" Ric stated, taking a small step towards me. I gripped the orb and reminded myself of the plan.

"I do," I whispered. I couldn't allow him to speak it. Hudson and Sebastian could never learn this. They'd already learned more than anyone else alive with Ric's fabulous description of my abilities.

"Do you know your father seeks you out?" Ric asked. Ice prickled my veins. He could never find me, I wouldn't live to see another sunrise. "I can protect you," Ric said, taking another small step towards me. My eyes flicked up and in his black depths I saw the end of my world. He would use me until I was drained dry. This had to end here, Ric knew too much. He would die here tonight, I couldn't allow the Order to question him. His eyes tightened as he read his own death in mine. I stepped forward and faked a trip. My hand grabbed the orb, and I flayed my arms for good measure. He lunged for me. Got ya. I smashed the orb on his head, the contents spilling down his face. I brought my knee up, nailed him in the balls and rolled him over my head. He sucked in a breath, inhaling the potion and grasped his crotch, his face twisted in agony.

"What have you done?" he growled at me.

"I just made the playing field even, asshole." Standing, I drew my leg back and prepared to introduce his face to my heavy boot. He grabbed it just before impact. He twisted my ankle taking me off guard, I tried to follow the momentum but I was a split second too late. I screamed as my bone snapped, white hot pain shooting to my brain. Birds shot from the trees and my body trembled with the need to release my true form. I could be healed in an instant and squash this bug to the ground. I would also paint a gigantic target on my back and be lucky to see the next sun rise. I glimpsed the protruding bone. I would survive. *Cora Roberts, one kick wonder.*

He was up and on me in a second, his hands wrapping around my throat. A roar split the air and a sabre-tooth tiger out of nightmares came barreling through the wall of creatures and hit Ric in his abdomen. They rolled onto the ground next to me. One creature reached down and clawed through Hudson's fur. The answering roar had me slapping my hands over my ears and turning towards the ground. The enormous cat was hurtled over my head. He shook his head and bared his teeth at the creature.

"Guard her," Hudson's deep growl came from the opposite side of the tiger. The pain was making me delirious. Because cats didn't talk. The cat bore down on me, paws the size of footballs stepped over me, a low insistent growl rumbling along his stomach. If I wasn't in agony, I might be in awe of the snowy fur. Ric barreled towards me, his eyes pinned on the awesome creature guarding me. Hudson burst through the creatures and tackled Ric to the ground. I looked up at the tiger and back at Hudson. If Hudson was there, then who the fuck was this? Ric threw a left hook at Hudson, he took it, the creature above me snarling in warning. Hudson pummeled Ric in the stomach, sending him back a few steps. Hudson wiped the blood from his lip with the back of his hand and glared at Ric.

Two of the circling creatures lurched and grabbed Hudson's arms. Again the tiger snarled. "Stay," Hudson growled. A low, angry rumble sounded above me.

"The mighty Principal of North America, brought down by a few creatures of the underworld. It makes me wonder where you acquired the mighty titles such as the Terror of Tennessee and the Louisiana Leviathan. What was the latest one? That's right, the South Carolina Savage." Ric gave a disappointed sigh. Hudson struggled in the creature's grip. I frowned. He wasn't trapped, he wasn't that weak. Hudson's gaze skirted to my thigh. Right, plan C. Except I couldn't freaking move.

Harry appeared between us, his shocked face quickly straightening after taking in the beast above me. "Sebastian has Maggie. He fought the creatures valiantly, and when they left in fear, he got her out. She's safe. Time to go."

"Time to die," I whispered.

Harry shook his head as my hand inched down my thigh. I gritted my teeth as every movement sent hot waves of pain through my body. I was trembling all over.

"Get up and let's go, Miss. Roberts," Harry stated.

"Not now, Harry," I muttered, eyeing Hudson. I was waiting for his signal. Hudson tilted his head, well shit. He gave a subtle nod of his head and launched himself out of the grip of the creatures. He rammed into Ric, whose ass hit the ground and skidded towards me. My hand gripped the handle of the dagger, I whipped it out and rolled, it passed through Harry and landed in Ric's chest. I jerked up and to the left. Ric convulsed, blood springing out of his mouth and his eyes suddenly cleared of the obsidian. His hand held mine, and I pushed deeper with a war cry. The life drained from him, the creatures surrounding us evaporated, whatever magic he'd used to bring them into existence died when he did. I rolled to my back, coming eye to eye with the tiger. He opened his mouth. I froze. Was I about to survive a psychotic man just to be eaten by a prehistoric, extinct creature? His tongue lolled forward, and he licked me from chin to forehead. Awesome. *Cora Roberts, beast tamer.*

Hudson scanned the area before his gaze assessed me. His eyes paused at my ankle. I couldn't look. "You're hurt," he muttered, stepping towards me. The cat rumbled above me, part warning, part greeting.

"Who the hell is this?" I asked. "Your brother?"

311

Hudson laughed and the beast over me finally stepped away and towards him. My hand twitched, and I had the absurd urge to reach up and stroke his fur. "Don't," Hudson said. I clenched my fist.

The beast loped to his side and brushed up against him. He disintegrated into the air... no, not the air; he was attaching himself to Hudson. I blinked and Hudson stood alone. Our eyes met, and he clenched his jaw. My mouth fell open, my pain dulled as I tried to join the dots together. Hudson bent down, scooped me up in his arms and began walking towards the car that was kicking up dust down the dirt road as it sped towards us. "He's you," I stated.

Hudson gave me one sharp nod. "I can separate from my beast form."

This was incredible, I'd never heard of that before. Ever. It didn't happen. Then again, sabre-tooth tigers weren't exactly roaming the woods either.

"Dave, the Doc and now you know this secret."

"I won't tell anyone," I muttered.

"I know you won't," he stated. Which meant he'd heard every single thing that Ric had said. I held his secrets, and he held mine. We wouldn't be silent because of trust. We would be silent because of fear.

"Cora," Sebastian shouted. I twisted my head around and found him launching out of the SUV and towards me. He ran his hand through his hair. Blood smeared his mouth. I frowned. Who had he fed from?

"Put her down, I'll heal her," Sebastian stated. Hudson's arms tightened around me a fraction. I tensed and black dots danced at the edges of my vision. I was losing blood.

"No, it's a broken ankle. She will survive."

"She's in pain, I need to heal her," Sebastian demanded.

"You've fed her your blood this week already. How is the urge going?" Hudson asked.

I frowned and fought through the brain fog. "Urge?"

"The more he gives you, the tighter the bond becomes. Two feedings in a short period might tip him over the edge."

I knew about the bond, but the rest? "Over the edge to what?"

"You never told her?" Hudson asked.

Sebastian looked at me, his eyes tightened. "It's not a concern."

"Told me what," I mumbled. I was about to lose consciousness, but I had to know what was going on.

Hudson bypassed Sebastian and waited at the rear door. "The urge to take your blood in return will claw at his soul, the more of his blood you have in your system. The harder it will be for him to resist."

"But if he drinks from me we will be mated," I whispered.

Sebastian opened the door, and Hudson slid into the rear seat with me in his lap. "I'll grab the body," Sebastian stated with a sigh. The door slammed closed. The trunk opened, and the car wobbled.

I looked in the front. Maggie was passed out in the passenger seat. "She's okay," Hudson muttered. A few seconds later, Sebastian hopped into the driver's seat and spun the car around. I slid and cried out as my ankle jostled. Bile shot up my throat and I regretted the liter of Gatorade.

"Careful," Hudson growled.

"Sorry, Cora. We'll be at the hospital in a matter of minutes. They will get this sorted for you."

I shook my head. "No, not the hospital. I can't go there."

"You need that bone plated and screwed into place," Hudson said, nodding towards my ankle.

"Can't Norbert do it?" I asked.

Hudson frowned at me. "We don't have that kind of setup."

"I do."

Hudson studied me; the pain could explain the tremble of fear in my body. I hoped. He dug in his pocket and pressed the phone screen, typing with just his thumb whilst his other hand secured me to him. The screen lit up a few seconds later. "He'll meet us at your home." I sighed, closed my eyes and let the darkness take me.

CHAPTER TWENTY

You can't pick your family.

I tried to turn over and groaned. My leg wouldn't cooperate. The heavy weight of the plaster kept me on my back, my least favorite sleeping position. The sun was just a whisper in the night sky. It had taken Norbert three hours to set my bone to his satisfaction, I'd been blacked out for the majority of it. Hudson had carried me to my bed not long after with instructions to sleep and heal.

I glared at the ceiling fan; I spent my life chasing healing sleep, and it was rare I got enough. Here I was plastered to the sheets and I couldn't even grab a nap. It was a new form of torture.

"Cora?" a masculine voice called out in the room. I jerked my head up and raised myself on my elbows. No fucking way.

"Ric, you murderous evil dick—get out of my house."

He focused a hard stare on me. "I don't understand why I'm here."

"Neither do I, because there's zero chance of me helping you gain peace."

Ric floated over and hovered at the end of the bed. He frowned at my plastered leg. "Did you hurt yourself?"

"No, you hurt me."

He dropped his head into his hands. "I don't understand. I was at the formal Spring ball, I came home… then I woke up here."

"The Spring ball was months ago, we are in the last weeks of summer."

"How is that possible? I need to get back to the Order, warn them something isn't right."

"Ric?"

His head shot up, and dark blue eyes bored into mine. He knew, he just couldn't accept it. "You're dead," I explained.

He shot to his feet and paced around my bed. "I'm not dead. I'm Ric Nicols, an elite of the Order. I can't be dead."

I flopped down onto my pillow. "You're telling me you don't remember murdering shifters and vampires over the last few months. Then trying to control me?"

"Why would I want to control you?"

I ran my hands over my face. This couldn't be happening. If someone had been pulling his strings, then I'd killed an innocent man. The Order was going to have my head for this. I could explain killing a murderous psychotic man on a rampage, but killing a man being used as a puppet... the President would demand better. She would have expected me to see through the bullshit, and it might just cost me my freedom.

"Why are you here?" I asked.

"I followed the light, right into your house and then to you. You're shiny like a beacon."

His body was probably on ice in my lab. He'd followed it and then the soul stone in the other room, the room I couldn't get to right now. I could try opening a portal here, but then where was I opening it to? I had never for one second thought I had a back door into heaven and was Ric

318

completely innocent? It could be a ruse. Ugh, my head hurt. "I can't deal with you right now," I told him. "I need to rest and heal, plus you nulled my magic. I need to get it back before I can do anything."

He bent over me, his brown spiky hair flopping forward. "I nulled your magic?"

"That's right, so you'll just have to hang out until I can sort out this mess. Harry and possibly Jennifer are around here somewhere, they are both ghosts—but you killed them."

"I didn't kill anyone," he gritted out. If he was acting, he needed an Oscar.

"Explain that to them. I need sleep." I yawned, conversations with the dead were exhausting, and me trying to pry apart what the hell was going on was sapping every morsel of energy I had left.

A week passed before my magic came trickling back, and with it renewed healing. Maggie and Rebecca brought me food and kept me company. Sebastian visited daily. Dave stopped by occasionally whilst Hudson remained absent.

By day ten I was out of bed, dragging the cast on my leg around and demanding Doctor Norbert. He removed the cast and gave me a set of crutches, declaring me a stubborn woman.

I had made it downstairs for the first time since that night. Rebecca sat in the parlor, brunch set out before her awaiting my arrival. I hobbled to the closest chair and flopped down in it with a heavy sigh. Healing was exhausting.

I scooped up a sandwich. "Update me," I said. She and Maggie had been running the day-to-day business of the bed and breakfast.

"Well, Doctor Norbert has seen your urgent cases. They all seemed content with him. The guests have arrived and departed as planned, with no issues. Bookings are up, and I persuaded Maggie to postpone the singles evening."

I nodded as I munched through another sandwich. The boundary wards clanged in my head. I winced, as much as it was needed, it was something I didn't miss. "Oh and–" she started. I put my finger up.

"Hold that thought," I said and grabbed my crutches. I hoisted myself up and made my way to the front door just as the house wards vibrated, an undercurrent of malice detected. Not against me, just in general. I flung the door open and came face to face with The President of The High Order of Elementals dressed in a navy power suit and matching six-inch heels. Not a single hair was out of place on her sleek silver bob. I held her shrewd emerald green gaze. The old bitch respected strength. If I showed a second of weakness, she would tear me to bits.

"Good morning, Madam President, welcome to Summer Grove House, I offer my assistance and hospitality to the Order." I worked on not gritting my teeth. It was a formal greeting that irritated me to the core.

She swept past me, three of her minions trying to follow. She turned and glared at them. They backed down the steps. "Shut the door, Cora, we need to talk."

I swung the door shut whilst balancing on my crutches. "Yes, Grandmother."

Eloise Roberts glided into the parlor and sat in the center of the largest sofa, Rebecca was nowhere to be found. Figures she'd leave me to the wolves. My grandmother whispered some words, and the room shimmered with a silencing spell. "You have been a busy girl."

I found my way back to the armchair and sat carefully, back straight, pose intact. "We had a situation, I handled it."

Over the last week, I'd decided that Ric was innocent. But that didn't change what had happened, and this woman could never learn that I could communicate with the dead. I'd be sequestered into the depths of The Order, never to be seen again. Over the years, my grandmother had made it clear the Order came before family. She leveled me with the Roberts' stare I both hated and loved. "You handled it? One of my most powerful elites is dead. How is that you handling it?"

"He was on a murderous rampage, many shifters had already become his victims, then he started on the vampires. Most of the shifters were pack, and the vampire was house."

Her left eyebrow twitched. "Does the Principal know?"

I nodded. "He does, as does the Crown Prince. They are satisfied with the outcome, there will be no retaliation."

Her green gaze bored into mine. "You have done well to manage the situation, I am proud."

Despite myself, I beamed inside. Making my grandmother proud was no simple feat. "Thank you."

"Of course you could have simply detained Ric and not killed him."

I arched an eyebrow at her. "He refused to come quietly."

"And the Principal and Prince, how much do they know about you?"

"They both now know I can perform retro reads."

She grimaced. "Do you expect them to share this information?"

I shook my head. "No." Because I trusted Sebastian, and I held one of Hudson's secrets.

"There will be a formal enquiry led by myself, I don't expect to find anything but a rogue elemental that turned psychotic and a woman who took charge and calmed a potential political catastrophe."

I nodded, and she relaxed her shoulders. The President had left the building and my grandmother was now in her place. She nodded towards my ankle. "How are you?"

"Healing," I stated.

"Good. You will need your strength for your task."

I stiffened. Very clever grandmother, lull me into a false sense of you doing me a favor before commanding one of your own. "What task?"

"You seem to have made beneficial alliances with the shifters and vampires. You are to be the official liaison between the three factions."

"What? No."

"You will report directly to me, I want to know everything that happens no matter how big or small. We need to build a more comprehensive picture of the factions."

She wanted to build a dossier to bulldoze them with if she felt the need. "I won't do it."

She tilted her head. "Consider it your punishment, I could launch a full inquiry led by Michael Glaister."

I grimaced. Michael Glaister or The Hound. He was the last person I needed digging into my business.

"Fine," I gritted out. This was just one plate to spin in my act. Rebecca appeared at the edge of the room with a tray of steaming cups. My grandmother grinned at her. She had a soft spot for the Vampire Princess, no doubt born from the fact she held a secret over the Vampire Royals having one of their own hiding out at her grandchild's residence.

My grandmother stood and waved Rebecca forward. I stood and steadied myself with the arm of the chair. "I can't stay for tea, I have other engagements in the area." She air kissed Rebecca, shooting me a hard look. I nodded and she snapped her fingers. The glittering spell burst from the walls and shimmered in the air before disappearing. She waltzed out of the room. The front door swung open, revealing one of her minions standing with their head bowed. She tutted like he was a disappointment and just like that the President of the Order exited my home and left me with a sour taste in my mouth.

I sighed, flopped back into my chair and massaged my temples. "So the other thing I had to tell you…"

Loud masculine shouts drifted through the open front door. What on Earth? I scrambled up on my crutches and began hobbling to the door. "Hold that thought," I told her. She let out a long-suffering sigh as I made my way to the porch and found the parking area in front of the stables stuffed full of trucks, random furniture and shifters.

"What did you do?" I whispered to Rebecca.

"Maggie rented out the stables," she muttered. "By the time I looked at the contract and found out who it was, it was too late."

"This can't be happening," I mumbled. The man in question snapped his head towards mine. He wiped his forehead with the shirt he'd whipped off at some point. My eyes did a scan of his bare chest. He was sex on a stick, and I couldn't have him living on my property.

He stalked towards me, leaving the other shifters to unload furniture and haul it into the stables. "He offered double," Rebecca said. My eyes tightened. What the hell are you up to, Hudson Abbot?

"Witch," he greeted as he came striding up my steps and came to a stop in front of me.

"I'll just be inside," Rebecca said and shot through the front door, swinging it closed behind her.

"Kitten, what are you doing?"

"Moving in," he stated with a tilt of his lips.

"Why? The pack house not good enough for your needs?"

"One of your own committed murder to get to you," he stated. My eyes narrowed. "That property that you rent to anybody is a liability, a weakness. I solved the problem."

"By moving in?"

"Yes, no need to thank me, I'm not a beast that likes pretty words."

"I wasn't about to thank you, in fact, I'd be happy if you just packed up your stuff and left."

He dug around his back jeans pocket and unfolded a sheet of paper. "In Clause 22 of the contract I signed here next to your signature, it clearly states the terms for which you can evict me. And I haven't broken those terms."

"You're not here to protect me, you're here to spy."

"You speak to the dead." I gritted my teeth and nodded. "Even when your magic is nulled." I gave him the hard assed Roberts' stare. He didn't even flinch. He pushed a thumb against his lip and took a step back. "I take it back, Cora, you are an interesting woman." Why did that sound like a threat rather than a compliment? He gave me a grin, all teeth, like he'd just heard me and turned away to help his minions unpack the new pack HQ. Oh boy.

THE ÆND

Thank you for beginning Cora and Hudson's journey... the next installment is planned for later this year.

If you want to stalk me you can find me here –
Facebook reader's group – Adaline's Warriors (where you will find a group of the most awesome, like-minded people who are currently sharpening their knives).

Instagram - @adalinewinterswriter (my main hangout because of all the amazing, supportive people there).

Email – adalinewinterswriter@gmail.com

Acknowledgments

Liberty and Zoe, for being the most awesome PA's and crisis managing my ass every day. I couldn't do this without you! If I posted something pretty on social media, chances are they did it.

Thank you to Anita for believing in this story so many months ago, and all your invaluable feedback and support.

Michaella, thank you for your support and alpha reading my raw story. Words can't describe how kind and invaluable you are.

Marsha, thank you for reading this and convincing me to publish it! Also, for your IT support. Zsuzsanna, thank you for helping get this book out to the world!

Tanya – thank you for the extra support – double beta reading and the puppy advice! Thank you to Shaun, Stephanie and Erica - my amazing beta readers. You are all awesome!

JoJo – thank you for your cheeky addition – happy birthday and let's hope this happens ;-)

To all the above, you are now stuck with my ass. Congrats.

To my daughter, life throws the most difficult obstacles at us, but these are trials we can face together. You are my inspiration every time you beat back a fear. Keep going, you got this. To my husband... three books in... who'd have thought? I love you, thank you for believing in the dream and in me.

Adaline x

P.S. Hudson is Liberty's – she licked him first... sorry everyone.

Whispers of the Dead: The Playlist

Hallucinate – Dua Lipa

In the Shadows – The Rasmus

Nothing Breaks Like a Heart – Mark Ronson (feat. Miley Cyrus)

Death of Me – PVRIS

I'll Follow You – Shinedown

Extraordinary – Clean Bandit feat. Sharna Bass

I Knew You Were Trouble – Taylor Swift

Moderation – Florence and the Machine

Take Care of You – Ella Henderson

Bury a Friend – Billie Eilish

Afraid of the Dark – The Unions

In Our Blood – Claie Guerreso

Monsters – Ruelle

Down to the Bottom – Dorothy

Because you Know – Becky Shaheen

Bring me to Life – Evanescence

When It's All Over – Raign

Let You Love Me – Rita Ora

Made in United States
North Haven, CT
19 May 2024

52708007R00202